Write Around Whidbey

BOOKS BY WHIDBEY WRITERS GROUP

Beneath the Rain Shadow (1994)

Beneath the Rain Shadow II (1996)

Beneath the Rain Shadow III (1999)

Take Our Words for Whidbey (2002)

Whispers in the Mist (2004)

Whidbey Connections (2007)

Whidbey Writes Again (2010)

Write Around Whidbey (2015)

Dedicated to

Kaye & Siouxy

Mary Katherine LaTorra Erickson
(1925-2012)

Suzanne Goodson Fulle
(1929-2015)

Contents

In Memoriam

Mike McNeff

MIKE MCNEFF *is a retired police officer and lawyer who started writing novels in 2009. He has been a resident of the Town of Coupeville on Whidbey Island since 2004. He draws on his law enforcement career and keen interest in history and current events for his stories. Mike is married to his wife Linda, and they have four grown children and seven grandchildren. His published works include* GOTU, Necessary Retribution, Hard Justice, *and several short stories.*

HOME

One

The timbers and ropes of the *Lady Washington* groaned as she leaned into a larboard tack to leave the Strait of Juan de Fuca. Seaman Sean O'Mara stood on the quarterdeck gazing at coastal bluffs and prairies bordered with rain forest. His interest lay directly down the strait from its entrance. Captain Gray had been ordered by the expedition commander, Captain Kendrick, to find the entrance to the strait, not explore it. Thus the reverse of course. Sean couldn't explain why he felt attracted to the bluffs of waving grass and green prairies so vivid against the azure sky. He just was. He deeply inhaled the sweet-tasting breeze for what he thought was the last time.

"You look like you've lost your best friend, Sean," Bob Haswell kidded.

"Oh, I just wanted to explore that coast down the strait."

"Aye, we all did. But orders are orders. Even if they come from Kendrick."

"I'm glad we be shut of that bastard," Sean spat.

"Quiet, Sean," Bob whispered. "Kendrick is still the commander of this expedition, and even though he ordered us transferred from the *Columbia* to the *Washington* he has allies on this ship that keep an eye out for him."

"I know, but Captain Gray keeps them in check."

"For now, but we're headed back to Nootka Sound to rendezvous with the *Columbia*, so keep your calm."

"Aye, Bob, I will."

Sean replayed the whole affair in his mind for the thousandth time. The men had been on the *Columbia* with Captain Kendrick, but at the Falklands, Kendrick unfairly demoted Sean from able seaman to ordinary seaman. Haswell, as third mate, objected to the demotion. The argument grew intense until Kendrick transferred Bob and Sean to the *Lady Washington*. It wasn't lost on both men that after they left, Kendrick promoted his son to third mate.

Sean's thoughts were interrupted by Neptune, an Alsatian Wolf Dog owned by Seaman Olsen. When Olsen wasn't beating the dog he ignored him. Sean liked the dog and played with him, trained him some, and shared his food with him. The dog rose up on his hind legs and greeted Sean, who gave out a hearty chuckle.

"Hey, my friend, how ye be today?" He rubbed behind Neptune's ears, something the big dog enjoyed.

Upon arriving at Nootka Sound the crew of the *Washington* found the Spanish had taken control of the area. Two British ships were impounded under Spanish control. Because the Kendrick expedition was American, the Spanish let them go with a warning about trespassing on their soil. The *Columbia* and *Lady Washington* sailed south for Clayoquot Sound.

On the second night at anchor in Clayoquot, Sean was standing third watch when Bob quietly came up to him.

"Bad news," Bob whispered. "Captain Gray has been ordered to take command of the *Columbia*. Kendrick is taking command of the *Lady Washington*. Gray is allowed to take me back to the *Columbia* with him, but not you. Watch yourself, Sean. Kendrick is after you."

Sean's shoulders slumped; 1789 wasn't turning out to be a good year.

Kendrick ordered the *Lady Washington* on a course for the entrance to the Strait of Juan de Fuca. He wanted to see it for himself before heading north. On the first day of the sail Kendrick had the first mate bring Sean before him.

"O'Mara, you are hereby demoted from ordinary seaman to landsman. You will follow the work orders of the first mate."

Sean looked at the first mate standing next to him, then back at the captain. "May I ask the captain what I've done to deserve this?"

A blow to the head knocked Sean to the deck. "You'll not challenge the captain, boy. You'll do as you're told," growled the mate.

Sean was immediately put to work scrubbing the decks, a job that normally took six to ten men. No one was allowed to help him. He worked on his knees twenty hours a day using dry sand and a holystone. Several men were detailed to follow him and sweep the sand off the decks, but Sean was forbidden to stand. On two occasions the mate accused him of working too slowly and beat him with a rope's end. Some of the crew risked punishment by slipping him food and grog occasionally, but it wasn't much. Neptune came to him once, but the mate kicked the dog away. By the fourth night Sean knew he had to get off the ship.

After a brief sail into the strait the *Lady Washington* anchored off the coast of Paacheena, the name the natives called the part of an island that projected out into the Strait of Juan de Fuca. The night was calm and quiet. Sean waited until he was sure everyone on the mess deck was asleep. He crept onto the main deck, his bloody knees screaming in pain. He checked to see if the lookout was awake. A deep rumbling snore encouraged him forward. Sean went to a rope locker. He lifted out a long bundle of oilcloth he had hidden, and tied it to his chest. He snuck in the shadows to the forecastle and climbed over the gunwale when Neptune came up.

"Ah, Nep ol' boy, I'll miss ye for sure," Sean whispered as he petted Nep's head. Then he slipped down the *Lady Washington's* anchor rode into the chilly sea. He gasped at the cold and the salt water biting his raw knees. The sea was black and Sean could barely make out the shore in the night made moonless by the clouds. He heard a splash behind him but didn't stop. Even in midsummer he wouldn't last long in the cold water. Something brushed his leg and he looked back to see Neptune, a sight that brought a smile to his lips. The companions swam together to freedom. Sean from Captain Kendrick, and Neptune from Seaman Olsen.

Sean fought the currents for what seemed an eternity. He could feel his strength ebbing, sapped by the cold water, the lack of food, and exhaustion. He willed himself to swim faster, hoping he would make shore with a burst of speed. A few minutes later the weapons wrapped in the oilcloth tied to his chest scraped the rocky bottom. He struggled to stand, but was knocked down by the waves. He forced himself back up and heard Neptune barking and whining. The dog was floundering. Sean took a few steps back and grabbed the big dog by the scruff of the neck, fighting his weakness and the undertow to cross the last ten yards to the shore. Once out of the water both he and Nep collapsed on the rock-strewn sand.

Sean lay shivering and drawing ragged breaths. Nep came to his feet and shook the sea off of himself…and onto Sean. Then he started licking the man's face with a worried whine. Sean rubbed Nep's ear.

"It's OK, mate. You're right; we have to get going." They must move, for as soon as the ship's crew found him missing they would send out a search party. If found, Sean would face even more severe punishment from Kendrick. He groaned as he rose to his feet and headed for the tree line. Once concealed by the trees he untied the oilcloth from his chest and removed the weapons that were again individually wrapped. He had a cutlass, a dirk, and a flintlock pistol with a powderhorn and ball. He unwrapped a smaller cloth soaked in oil and wiped everything down and loaded his firearm. He wasn't going back.

Sean moved quietly. Although each step caused his knees to protest, it felt good to be upright. He had to avoid contact with the natives here. At first the sailors and natives were friendly and conducted trade. But Kendrick treated the natives poorly and they had turned violent. Although Sean felt the same way the natives did about Kendrick he knew they wouldn't understand that. They would kill him. He moved along the coast in the tree line. The darkness made for slow going, but the movement warmed him. Finally the sun began to light the low grey clouds in the east, allowing him to see enough to move faster.

He came to a stream and stopped so he and Nep could drink the clear, cold water. He pulled a piece of sodden salt pork from his pocket and broke it in half, giving one portion to Nep. The dog took it in one gulp. Sean pulled the dog to him and rubbed behind his ears.

Suddenly Sean could hear voices, and then shots mingled with the zip of arrows in flight echoed in the forest. Sailors against natives. Both sides of the fight were his enemies. He ran for the interior of the dark emerald-and-jade rain forest. A long sprint came to an abrupt halt as he startled two natives. Sean charged them as one lifted his bow.

The native with the bow started to pull back his bowstring.

Sean slashed with his cutlass. The blade sliced through the man's shoulder into his chest, and his scream reverberated down Sean's spine. Sean pulled the blade and turned to a growling Nep, who had the other native down as the native tried to club him. Sean plunged his cutlass into the native's heart.

Sean felt burdened with deep regret for having to kill the two natives. His heart pounded, and his dry mouth made it difficult to swallow. "C'mon, Nep. We have to keep going," he croaked. They moved northwest at a trot, to try to get to other side of the island.

The companions alternated running and walking. The cloud layer burned off and Sean began to warm up in the bright sun. They stopped for water occasionally and Sean picked some blueberries and crabapples to eat. He felt a renewed strength. Nep ate the last of the salt pork.

They topped a hill on the east side of the island as the sun began to drop to the horizon. Below them lay a harbor with a large native village of long houses and smaller shelters next to the water. Sean could see many different sizes of canoes on the beach and knew he could handle the smaller ones. Little dogs ran in between the legs of the natives. Some had white fur and some looked shaved. He knew the dogs were natural to the island and the natives made blankets from their fur. Sean backed off the crest and settled down in a stand of trees to wait for nightfall, mulling over the problems of slipping into the village.

Two

Sean moved carefully in the moonlit night. He came to the coast north of the village and led Nep to a large tree. "Stay."

Nep lay down and looked up with worried eyes.

Sean rubbed the dog behind his ears and laid his pistol wrapped in oil next to him. "It's all right, boy," he whispered. "I'll be back as soon as I can. I can't risk those dogs catchin' your scent."

Sean started walking toward the village. Just as he rounded the last bend before the bay he slipped into the water and swam for the canoes. Thank God the water was warmer on this side of the island, but it was still chilly. When he came close to the village he submerged until his hands touched the bottom and he looked up. He spied a smaller canoe and half-floated, half-crawled over to it.

Sean grabbed the end of the canoe and pulled just enough to get it to move. The bottom scraping on the sand sounded like thunder to him. His heart thumped against his chest, his senses alert and sharp. Nothing seemed to stir in the village until one of the little dogs appeared at the water's edge. The dog looked at him for a moment.

Sean stopped breathing, every muscle tense.

The little dog lifted his leg, squirted, then turned and walked away.

Sean let out a long breath, worked the canoe into the water, and guided it back to where Nep waited. He beached the canoe and looked for the tree where he had left his dog. But in the moonlight all the trees looked the same. He cursed himself for not marking the beach.

"Hey, Nep. It's me boy. C'mon out," he whispered. Nep didn't appear. Sean looked for as long as he dared. He must get away from the island. He made his way back to the canoe. Tears brimmed in his eyes. Not only had he lost his pistol; he'd lost his only friend as well. As he got closer to the canoe he heard thumping behind him. He drew his cutlass and spun around only to see Nep standing there, his tail wagging, the wrapped pistol in his mouth.

Sean let out a great whoosh of air. "Nep, ye old salty dog." He wrapped his arms around his friend as Nep licked his face.

"Get in the boat, mate." Nep jumped in the canoe and Sean's heart was happy. He pushed the craft into the water, climbed in, and headed for those beckoning bluffs to the east.

Sean paddled with strong strokes, thankful for the bright moonlight that helped him navigate. At daybreak he felt the tide turning against him. The current threatened to carry him back to Paacheena. The tides changed twice a day in this part of the world. He had to get to shore and wait for the next incoming tide. He thrust his paddle into the water and pulled hard and fast toward the nearest land, the first island east of Paacheena. His arms ached and his breath came short and quick, but fear kept his arms in motion. He felt his heart would burst until he saw the rocky bottom. He jumped out of the canoe and pulled it the rest of the way to shore.

He collapsed on the sand. Nep lay next to him. A gentle breeze played over him as he looked at the white ships of cloud sailing by in the vast blue above him. Exhaustion and lack of sleep began to take hold. Sean drifted...

Nep's urgent bark jolted Sean. He jumped to his feet in an instant to see a canoe with four natives headed for him.

"Neptune, in the canoe!"

Sean pushed it into the water, his mind taking stock of the conditions at lightning speed. It appeared to be slack tide. Four natives could paddle much faster than Sean. His mind worked on a plan while his oar cut into the water.

An arrow whizzed past his head. The natives were closing fast.

He rotated his canoe to face them. An arrow hit the canoe deck in front of him. Then with a sickening *thunk,* an arrow struck his thigh. The native canoe was coming straight at him. He pulled his pistol, aimed, and pulled the trigger. A loud report and a large cloud of smoke launched a lead ball. The shot hit the first native kneeling sideways in the canoe, tumbling him into the water. The ball appeared to go through him and hit the next man, knocking him back against the third native, who struggled to keep his wounded friend in the craft. Their canoe floated next to Sean. His cutlass flashed in the sunlight, slashing the arm of the third man, who screamed. Sean's intent was to wound, not to kill.

The fourth man stared at Sean, his eyes sick with fear. Sean pointed to Paacheena. "Go!"

The last oarsman nodded furiously and

paddled away, turning his canoe back toward their home. He slowed to look at the body of his fellow brave floating in the water. The oarsman and the wounded third man struggled to get their friend into the canoe.

Sean could see that they were having trouble. He paddled over to them. At first they were frightened, but Sean held up his empty hands. He pointed to the man in water and then to their canoe.

They nodded.

The three of them were able to maneuver the first man into the canoe. Sean was relieved when the man moaned. At least he was still alive.

Sean backed his canoe away from the natives while they turned their canoe around.

The oarsman turned around and looked at Sean. He raised his open hand.

Sean returned the gesture.

The oarsman started paddling home with his wounded fellow warriors.

Sean leaned against the side of his canoe and groaned with relief. He inspected his wound. The arrow was stuck in the outer thigh. He broke off the feathers and with a pain-filled growl pushed the arrow through. He tore off a strip of his shirt and bandaged the wound. He gazed skyward and smiled.

"Thank Ye for me Irish luck!"

He set off at a steady pace. Soon his speed increased with the incoming tide. His leg throbbed, but the pain faded with each stroke closer to his goal.

The bright sunlight and nature's brush created a tapestry of greens, browns, and blues all around him. Majestic snow-capped mountains towered above him and in the distance. Otters swam along and played around the canoe in the sunlit water. He laughed when Nep barked at them. Sean inhaled deeply. He had discovered Paradise.

By the end of slack tide he made shore north of the bluffs and prairie he sought. He had no choice but to land there or he would be caught in the outgoing tide. When he brought the canoe onto shore, schools of salmon swam around him. As hungry as he was he needed to slake his raging thirst. He knew Nep needed it too.

The rain forest came right up to the beach. He let Nep take the lead, hoping he would be able to smell fresh water. Nep found a deer trail, a good sign. When they crossed a path made by humans Sean pulled his dog to him and held him close while he listened. Nep's ears moved also, but soon his tail started wagging so Sean decided to move ahead.

A short time later they came to a small lake nestled in a pocket of the thick rain forest. Nep smelled the water and then started drinking. Sean bent down. The pain in this thigh and knees pulled a gasp from his lungs. He took in gulps of cool, delicious water. They drank their fill and rested for a moment while Sean cleaned his wound and battered knees. His stomach started to growl and he remembered the salmon. They headed back to the beach.

Silvery salmon sparkled in water off the edge of the shore. This time Sean was delighted to wade into the water. Salmon hurtled by, some hitting his legs. He made several attempts to stick a salmon, but only caught frustration. To his chagrin Nep came out of the water with one and dropped the flopping fish on the shore. He played with it for a moment and then went back into the water.

Not to be outdone Sean finally speared a salmon. He headed back to shore and saw Nep had caught another one. He petted his dog with a chuckle.

"Well, mate, it appears you're a mite better fisherman than me."

Sean carried their catch to trees and started to gather wood. Nep saw what he was doing and started bringing in sticks and branches also. Each trip the dog made, the wood he brought got larger and larger. Sean grabbed his friend and hugged him, letting laughter from deep within him spill out. It felt good. A small fire started with flint and stone was soon burning in a little depression in the forest to hide it from dangerous eyes. While Sean waited for the fire to burn down for cooking he made a poultice out of Stinging Nettle he found and applied it to his wound and his knees.

When the fire burned down he put the cleaned salmon on upright sticks to cook, as he had seen the natives do. When the fish were done the two companions ate a great feast, Sean carefully feeding Nep salmon free of bone. The exhausted pair settled in for the night as the setting sun set the sky ablaze with orange, blue, and purple hues.

Three

At the first slack tide of the morning Sean and Nep paddled toward the bluffs. A sea breeze played with the trees against the welcoming glow of the rising sun. As they drew near their goal Sean heard a woman yelling. His eyes swept the area and caught a glint of sunlight off the wet bottom of an overturned canoe. The woman clung to it.

He paddled over to her and held his hand out. She pulled back, yelling and pointing to the water under the canoe with a tearful face. Sean suddenly understood and jumped into the water, with Nep following him. He saw a young boy under the canoe whose foot was caught in a decorative cutout. He worked the boy free and brought him to the surface.

Sean didn't stop to get the boy into the canoe. He swam with the boy to the shore, carried him to the beach, and laid him on his belly. Then he pumped the boy's back. He kept pumping as the woman came ashore with his canoe. She ran to the boy's side, talking to him and tearfully stroking his face.

Sean pumped until frustration streaked his face. Just as he thought he was too late, the boy coughed. His body lurched and sea water spurted from this mouth and nose. Sean picked the boy up by his midsection and held him bent over until the water stopped coming. He laid the boy down.

The boy started crying and the woman comforted him. Nep licked the boy's face, and that seemed to calm him down. The crying stopped.

A few minutes later the woman sat back on her haunches and tried to tell Sean something. After some impromptu sign language and drawings in the sand Sean figured out that the boy was her brother. The woman tried to lift the boy. Sean touched her arm and motioned that he would carry him. She stepped back and Sean took the boy into his arms. The woman pointed north and kept saying the word "Bu-tsads-a-lee." Sean nodded and they started walking across the prairie. A gentle breeze seemed to sing a soft song through the grass and trees, lulling the boy to sleep.

After walking a while Sean started to limp and the woman pointed to Sean's leg. His wound was bleeding again. Her eyes met his and something stirred inside him. She smiled, said something, and took off running.

Sean watched her as she went. *That be a real woman, all right.*

He limped in the direction she travelled and soon she brought a group of natives, concern etched on their faces. An older man walked forward, nodded to Sean, and took the boy from his arms. The natives gathered around the man with the boy and continued north. Sean watched them go, turned, and began to walk back to the bluffs, waves of sadness and loneliness washing over him. The woman ran up behind him, took his arm, and turned him to follow the others.

She pointed to her chest and said, "While-squi."

Sean pointed to himself and said, "Sean."

While-squi smiled and repeated his name. She put his arm over her shoulders to help him walk. Her touch brought warmth and comfort to Sean.

Joseph Whidbey, the sailing master of the *HMS Discovery*, climbed a hill with his small party from the cove where his jolly boat lay. As he started further inland, natives approached him. One of the natives was a woman holding a child of about two years who appeared to be part white. The woman was again with child.

She stepped forward. "Welcome."

"Thank you," Whidbey said. "How do you come to speak English?"

"Ye come. I show ye." After they had walked a short distance a white man and a native boy stepped out of the trees. A large dog was with them. The woman walked toward the man and stood next to him. The dog put himself between Whidbey and the family before him.

"I believe you would be Sean O'Mara?"

Sean nodded.

"And that would be Neptune."

"Are ye looking to take me back?"

Whidbey smiled. "No. I bring greetings from Mr. Haswell. I met him in the Falklands. He asked that if I came across you to say he wishes you and Neptune well, and for you to rest easy. The company you were working for has no interest in punishing you for jumping ship." Whidbey looked around at the beauty surrounding him. "What is this place called?"

"This place is called Bu-tsads-a-lee, which means Snake Place. You're on an island called Tscha-kole-chy."

"You've come to a beautiful place, Mr. O'Mara."

Sean put his arm around his wife's shoulders. "I'd be grateful if ye'll not record in your logs that ye found Nep and me here. But if ye ever see Mr. Haswell again, please tell him we're very well. We're home."

Historical Note

Although Captain Vancouver is credited with finding the Great Northwest in 1792, the reality is that Spanish, Russian, British, and American merchant ships were plying the area years before Vancouver and the *HMS Discovery*. As indicated in this story, the Strait of Juan de Fuca had already been discovered by Europeans. British fur trader Charles William Barkley named the strait after the Greek explorer in 1787. It was widely known to other mariners by that name.

Captain Kendrick commanded an expedition commissioned by a Boston syndicate led by merchant Joseph Barrell. While Kendrick's seamanship abilities were known to be excellent, history does not reflect kindly on his leadership qualities. Mr. Robert Haswell was the third mate on board the *Columbia* and did get involved in a dispute with Kendrick over the disciplining of a seaman. As a result he was transferred to the *Lady Washington*, the other ship in the expedition under the command of Captain Gray, a more respected captain. Kendrick's son was promoted to fill Haswell's position. Later, Kendrick changed ships with Gray and allowed Gray to take Haswell with him.

Kendrick's attitude also caused strife between him and natives of Vancouver Island, which led to violence. This occurred two years after the setting of this story, however, on a second expedition to the area.

John Kendrick sailed the *Lady Washington* on expeditions to East Asia and the Sandwich Islands. In

1794, after helping a Hawaiian chief win a battle against another chief, Kendrick ordered a thirteen-gun salute for the British ship *Jackal,* which had also participated in the battle. The *Jackal* replied with a similar salute. Unfortunately, one of the *Jackal's* guns was loaded with grapeshot, which raked the captain's table on the deck of the *Washington,* killing Kendrick and several other men.

Robert Haswell served on the *Columbia* under Captain Gray for several years, rising to the position of first mate. In 1797, during the Quasi-War with France, he was commissioned in the U.S. Navy as a lieutenant and served with distinction. In 1801 he was given leave from the Navy to take the command of the merchant ship *Louisa* for an expedition to the northwest and the East Indies. The *Louisa* never returned, and its fate and that of Robert Haswell remain unknown.

Joseph Whidbey landed on Whidbey Island in July 1792. He completed his voyage with the *HMS Discovery* and went on to a long and distinguished career as a naval engineer in England until his retirement in 1830. He died in 1833.

As for Sean O'Mara and Neptune: Well, it is said that the sea breeze weaves an independence and perseverance through the populace and canines of the town of Coupeville on Whidbey Island not unlike the traits in those two spirits. There are whispers that on a quiet summer night on Snakelum Point you just might hear the ancient songs of the Canoe People, with one voice exhibiting a bit of an Irish brogue.

Avis Rector

*Whidbey Island has been home to **AVIS RECTOR** all her life. She and her husband, both retired teachers, enjoy life on their cattle farm. Gardening and walks on the beach are her favorite hobbies. She is the author of the children's book,* Carl Helps on the Farm, *and a novel,* Pauline, A New Beginning on Whidbey Island.

GUS AND HILDA

My father loved to tell stories, and each time he told the same story it got better than the last time he had told it. Back in the old days, company often dropped by on Sunday afternoons. I remember one particular time when I was confined to the house with a sore foot, Grace and Harvey Sellers came to visit.

Dad had them sit on the big maroon couch in front of the fireplace, and after they had talked about the weather and the kids, my mother said she would go to the kitchen to make coffee and cake, or maybe it was pie. Anyway, Dad stoked the coals in the fireplace and threw on another log. Eager to entertain, he pulled up his rocking chair, leaned forward, rested his elbows on his knees, and asked the guests if they had heard the story about Gus and Hilda.

Harvey said, "Nope, not that one." I guess Grace

didn't want to hear the story — maybe she had heard it before—because she got up and went out to the kitchen with my mother. So Harvey settled back into the couch and Dad began:

Back before the Deception Pass Bridge was finished in 1935, there was this older German couple, see. They came across on the little ferry in their Ford truck loaded high with all their stuff. Hilda – that was her name – was a tall, skinny kind of woman with long arms and legs. She always wore her hair in a tight bun at the back of her neck. Gus was a short, stocky man with a thick brushy moustache and bald head, and didn't talk hardly at all, just let his wife do all the talking with her broken English. She'd go on and on about why they left Germany, and the trip over on the boat, and how they had not liked New York.

They found a piece of land out in Cornet. That's not far from the bridge, see, and if you climb up Goose Rock and look down toward Ducken Road, you can see the trees on the hill. That's where they took over an old abandoned house. They had a lot of fixing to do, but they were hard workers and got the place looking pretty good.

Gus started raising chickens and bought a cow. There was a spring, probably a hundred yards or so from the house, and Gus got tired of carrying water. He scolded Hilda when he thought she used too much. One day he said he would dig a well. His neighbors made fun of him, saying the ground was too rocky. He was a stubborn man and didn't listen.

Dad cleared his throat, looked at the fire, and then back at Harvey.

Anyway, Gus, he found a place a short way from the house and started scratching around with his pickaxe to loosen the rocks from the clay soil. He stopped sometimes and wiped the sweat from his brow with his red bandanna and asked his wife for a glass of her homemade root beer. He was a strong fella, and some days worked until dark.

Neighbors came by once in a while. They teased him, saying he'd never reach water. Gus paid no attention to them, and kept swinging his pickaxe and digging until he stood knee-deep in the hole.

The time came when he couldn't angle the shovel high enough to put the dirt in the wheelbarrow, see, so he just threw it out and it piled up, making the sides higher and higher. Dirt and rocks rolled back down into the hole. He had Hilda help by raking the dirt away from the edge, but then he couldn't throw the dirt up and out of the hole. He explained to Hilda that he'd tie a rope to the handle of a bucket and she would pull it up and dump it into the wheelbarrow.

That worked for a while, until he had dug so deep, see, that he couldn't get in and out of the hole. He started using a ladder. After he climbed down, Hilda pulled it up so he had room to work. He kept digging, and she kept pulling up the bucket of dirt.

See, Hilda had made friends with the neighbor ladies, and one day she told Gus she wanted a day off to ask them over for afternoon coffee. He told her OK, he'd take a few hours off and go to town. That evening she made phone calls to the ladies.

A few days later they were working in the well when Hilda remembered it was Friday. "Oh, mein

Gott! Oh, mein Gott! The ladies are coming today!" she called down to Gus. "The ladies are coming! I be right back."

Dad leaned back in his chair and laughed, his brown eyes shining, and said, "She had quite an accent. It sounded kind of funny."

Well, Hilda let the bucket down to Gus and rushed into the house to mix up a cake. After putting it in the oven, she ran out and hauled up a bucket of dirt. Back and forth she went, checking the cake, tidying the house, hauling up a bucket, emptying out the dirt, letting the bucket down to Gus, and then going back to the house. When she heard a car coming up the hill, she let an empty bucket down to him, rushed into the house, and took off her apron ready to greet her company. The ladies started their chatter the way women do when they get together, and Hilda took them into the house.

Dad looked at Harvey to see if he understood what might be coming, and satisfied that he did, continued.

Poor Gus, forgotten in the well, yelled and yelled to no avail. He turned the bucket upside down, sat on it, and waited. Water seeped from the gravel seams down the sides and puddled at his feet. He tried digging steps into the wall, but the loose gravel fell out. He sat on his bucket again and rested his chin on his chest. The afternoon slipped away. Poor Gus had almost dozed off when he heard the starting of a car motor. He stood up, put his hands to his mouth, and called, "Hilda! Hilda!" Again and again he yelled.

After her guests drove away, Hilda went back to the house. She carried her pretty china teacups and cake plates to the sink and thought about the tidbits of gossip she would tell Gus. "Oh, mein Gott! Oh, mein Gott! Poor Gus! I left him in the well!" She ran out of the house, legs a-flying. She reached the hole and called down, "Gustave, are you down there?"

Gus stood up from his overturned bucket, put his hands on his hips, looked up, and declared, "Woman! Where do you think I am? Do you think I sprouted wings? Put down that ladder!"

She called down to him, "Oh, my poor Gus. I'm sorry."

He yelled up, "Damn it, woman, sorry isn't good enough!"

Dad laughed, took off his glasses, wiped his eyes, and told the rest of the story.

"Gustave, if I down the ladder, will you be good to me?"

Well, after a few dozen cuss words, he promised to be good, and she lowered the ladder. It was a long time before he would talk to her.

Dad got up and grabbed the poker to stoke the fire.

Harvey asked, "Did he ever finish the well?"

"No, he gave up on the well, and a few weeks later he sold the place and they moved off the island."

There is a trail on the southeast side of Deception Pass Bridge that leads to the top of Goose Rock. At 484 feet in elevation, it is the highest point on Whidbey Island. From there Mount Baker, the Olympic mountains, the San Juan Islands, and Vancouver Island are all visible. Evergreens obscure a view of where Gus and Hilda had lived.

BUD AND BUTCH

Part One: The Ninety-Seven-Seconds Rule

Bud and Butch lived with their ma in the small town of Hicksville, Arkansas. They took small jobs now and then, earning just enough to keep their house and buy a few necessities. Sitting on the back stoop one day, Butch, paring his toenails with his jackknife, said, "Hey, Bud, I want to drive the truck."

"You know the rule, Butch."

"Yeah, but just this one time can't I be the ruler?"

"Don't know that you know how to be the ruler."

"You could teach me, Bud."

"Yeah, but where would that get me? Don't know if you're teachable, Butch."

"Just once, Bud. Come on. What do you say?"

"I'll think about it."

"You got to learn to ride the bike first."

"Yep. That's the rule."

"Well, there's one thing you was first at and I didn't give a hoot."

"What was that, Butch?"

"Chicken pox!"

"Yeah, those about done me in."

"How come Ma always gives you the biggest and bestest steak or anything that's good?"

"You know, Butch, the ninety-seven-seconds rule."

"I hate that rule."

"Can't be helped, Butch. You had nine months

to think about it, but you pushed me out of Ma's belly first. A whole ninety-seven seconds before you climbed out."

Part Two: The Inheritance

One day a lawyer found Butch lollygagging around the back stoop and handed him a sheaf of papers. After looking at the first page, Butch called, "Hey, Bud!"

Bud came out of the house, letting the screen door slam. "What do you want?"

"Guess these are for you," said Butch, holding up the papers. "Ninety-seven-seconds rule."

Bud read through the papers. "Butch, it seems our uncle, the one that moved out to Washington, up and died and left us some money and a piece of land out there."

Butch asked, "The uncle that moved to Dug-a-la Bay on an island?"

"Yeah, Uncle Elmer." Bud held out the paper and pointed with his finger to Whidbey Island. "He had a little farm."

"What are we gonna do with it? Sell it?"

"Naw, don't want to do that," said Bud. He rubbed his red-stubble beard and looked at Butch.

"Want to be a farmer?"

That took Butch by surprise, as never having lived on a farm, neither knew much about animals or raising crops. Thinking about it, he kicked at a round rock in the dirt and when it stopped **moving**, kicked it again.

Bud watched the rock roll around a bit and then said, "Well, what do you say?"

"We better go look at what we got," said Butch.

"Yeah," said Bud. "We'll load up our stuff and take a little trip to see what we got."

"We better tell Ma. She won't like us leaving her here."

"Guess we'll just have to take her with us." When their ma heard about their plans, she said she didn't want to go traipsing across the United States to some wilderness, and would likely stay with her sister in Hicksville.

After several days travelling, Bud parked at a turnout on the north side of Deception Pass Bridge. "Wake up, Butch. I'm gonna stretch my legs and take a walk to have a look down at the water. Come on."

Looking down at the swirling whirlpools, Butch said, "Don't like this, Bud. Too scary. Let's go see our property."

"I'm about wore out, Butch. You slept most the way while I had to keep my eyes open. I'm gonna park here for a bit and get a little sleep-eye. You can eat crackers and peanut butter if you're hungry."

When the sun came shining through the fog in the morning, Butch shook Bud awake. "Come on, brother. I'm rarin' to go see our property at Dug-a-la Bay."

"Butch, I told you, it's a Indian name. Say *Dugwala*."

"Dugualla?"

"Yeah, you got it. Bring out that map and find Uncle Elmer's farm at Dugualla Bay."

"After a few stops to ask directions and a few turn-arounds, Bud drove down a dusty road to their property. They got out and standing by the truck, looked at the buildings, all in disrepair.

"Don't look like much," said Butch. "The door on that barn is just hangin' there all crooked, and the windows are all broke out. There ain't even no house. Looks like the one that was here burned down. Just a chimney left. Don't have any place for us stay."

"Just have to sleep out 'til we fix a place in the barn," said Bud.

"How we gonna keep any animals?" asked Butch.

"First off, we're gonna put a gate on that fence over there so they won't get out. Anybody with a brain knows you gotta have tight fences."

"We never had any experience doing any of that, Bud. How you fixin' to be a farmer?"

"Well, Butch, there are certain things the ninety-seven-seconds ruler knows. One is you have to ask for help."

"Who you gonna ask?'

"Other farmers. I'll start by introducing us to that neighbor just down the road. Might as well go talk to him right now."

"I'm coming with you."

Part Three: Becoming Farmers

Ned Brickly, delighted to learn that someone would be taking over the run-down property, got all puffed up giving advice to the boys and volunteered to check up on them to make sure they did things just right.

The brothers followed Ned's advice, doing

repair work on fences and cleaning out the old barn. One morning Bud said, "When we were at the Farmer's Co-op buying that fencing wire, I heard tell there's a sale down by Freeland, Butch."

"Gonna buy us some animals?"

"Yep. First off, we're gonna buy us a cow and a pig."

"Gotta have sheep," said Butch.

"Yep," Bud agreed. "We'll have some of them, too. Might as well go now so we can get there early and get the pick of the crop."

The boys enjoyed talking with the farmers and looking at the animals. They thought they spent their money wisely by buying a pregnant cow with a calf by its side.

"That's what you call a three-in-one package," said Bud. "We know a good deal when we find one."

"How we gonna get them home?"

"I thought of that and asked Brickly to haul them in his trailer. He said he'll do it. He's got an old bred sow we can buy. Won't be long and we'll have us a litter of piglets."

"If we're gonna have a farm, we gotta have chickens," said Butch.

"Yep, you're right on the money there. We'll get those and maybe a couple goats, too."

Butch reminded Bud that to have a bona fide real farm they needed a few sheep. Bud said, "Yep, matter a fact, I did agree to that." A few days later they bought a ram and two ewes from a farmer down the road.

"And Bud, there's one more thing I've been thinking about."

"You do a lotta thinking, Butch. What is it this time?"

"Did you notice something about all those farmers at the sale barn? They all wore those bib overalls. We gotta get some."

"Next time we're in town we'll stop at the Farmer's Co-op, Butch."

"And those red neckerchiefs like they have sticking outta their back pocket, too."

"OK, Butch, if that's what it takes to make you a real farmer."

Part Four: Turkey Talk

Butch sat on a stump picking itchy burdock burrs out of his socks one evening. "Hey, Bud, we ain't got no turkeys. A farm ain't a farm without turkeys."

"We got enough to do around here without having a bunch of gobblers."

"Bud, I gotta have a turkey for Thanksgiving. Wouldn't be Thanksgiving without a big fat drumstick to chomp into."

"All right. You go find us some turkeys. We'll have to get some wire to fence them in, or put them with the chickens."

Butch asked around about turkeys and learned about a turkey farmer over in the next county.

"We'd have to go across that Deception Pass Bridge, Butch."

"I'll just close my eyes and you can tell me when to open them."

So Bud drove their truck and enjoyed the view

from the bridge while Butch kept his hands over his eyes. They found the turkey farmer, bought a few poults, and brought them home in a gunny sack.

Butch dumped the turkeys out of the sack. The chickens put up a cackling fuss. The poults bunched up in a corner of the coop. Butch tried to get them to mingle with the hens and rooster, but they kept crowding back into a corner.

Bud said, "They'll smother each other all bunched up like that. Let's take them to that other little building."

The young turkeys settled down in their coop. Butch put mash in their tray and gave them fresh water. He liked watching the chickens when they drank. They put their heads up and kind of let the water run down inside their throats, but he never saw the poults drink.

"Bud, I'm worried about my turkeys; they ain't drinking no water. I'm going over to Brickly and ask him."

"Butch," said Ned, "turkeys are about the dumbest birds on earth. You have to teach them. Throw a few marbles in their trough."

The downy-feathered poults went after the bright colorful balls and learned to drink, but Butch had one more worry and told Bud: "The turkeys don't roost like the chickens do. I'll go talk to Brickly. He knows all the answers."

"Well, Butch," said Ned, "they don't have enough sense to know how. You'll have to teach them."

"How do I do that?"

"Think about it. You'll figure it out."

Butch thought a lot about how to teach his turkeys to roost on the horizontal poles and told Bud his plan. "You have to help me, Bud. We have to show them."

After he said no a couple of times, Bud finally gave in and said he would help.

One night Ned noticed Bud's truck parked by the turkey house and went over to see if everything was all right. He opened the coop door and yelled in, "What are you doing in the dark?"

Bud called back, "It's my turn helping Butch teach his turkeys how to roost."

Ned turned on the light. There sat Bud, squatting on the roosting poles, with a turkey sitting on each side of him.

SANDRA MCGILLIVRAY ORTGIES *was born in British Columbia and grew up in West Vancouver by the sea. Moving to San Francisco where she met Don was the start of rewarding years of family travels with the Air Force, stateside and in Europe. While English was Sandra's favorite subject at Texas Lutheran University, it wasn't until she enrolled in journalism electives and sold her first travel article to a Northwest magazine that she was hooked! Short stories, articles, and poetry remain her writing focus. As much as the Ortgies enjoy their continued travels, they are always happy to come home to Whidbey Island and their Coupeville community.*

2014 COUPEVILLE ARTS & CRAFTS FESTIVAL 50TH ANNIVERSARY

Connie felt that same anticipation each year as she and Alex came around the Coveland Street bend near the post office. Double rows of white tents stretched for over two blocks to Main Street. Hanging baskets of pink petunias and multicolored banners were placed at regular intervals along Coveland, accenting the festival scene. This same setup was duplicated one block north along Front Street, and the combined effect never failed to make Connie appreciate that they had chosen Whidbey Island with all its summer events as their home.

Alex swung into the post-office parking lot where "10 minutes only" signs had been set up for the duration of the festival. "Take your time, Connie. I've got a bunch of errands to run in Oak Harbor. Give me a call when you're ready, and I'll pick you up here."

"Let's have a late lunch up the hill at the festival food vendors and listen to live music for a while when you get back. Maybe the wine and beer garden too?"

Alex knew that Connie liked to take her time poking around the booths and talking with the artists and vendors. Connie knew that Alex could cover a 200-tent festival in about twenty minutes, so it was with some relief that they both made their own plans for the day.

Connie started out on her familiar circuit, enjoying the walk in the sunshine. The remarkable July weather of summer 2014 was holding into August, and even at this 10 A.M. opening time a steady stream of people were arriving for the festivities. She looked forward to seeing the new vendors and the many returning vendors who claimed the same spot each year. These vendors would store an item she purchased until she was ready to pick it up.

The Festival Committee tent featured a special display of photos with detailed captions through each decade, honoring their 50th Anniversary. The festival started in 1964 as a way to showcase local artists and rejuvenate the town. Continued growth each year saw hundreds of artists from all over the country participating, and thousands of people were expected again this year.

Michele Kempees, the 2014 featured artist, painted an endearing poster of a small child who was also painting a poster, which was replicated on sage-green T-shirts. Connie decided this was one she had to have. She and Alex used posters that had appealed to them from previous festivals to decorate the verandah room of their B&B, *Lanterns*. A T-shirt and a poster were her first buys of the morning.

Rounding the corner at Coveland and Alexander, she could see the tall masts of *Lady Washington* and *Hawaiian Chieftain*. The visiting sailing ships were roped to each other and to the end of the Coupeville Wharf for the duration of the festival, flags flying. These ships offered afternoon and evening sailing tours on their schedules. Over the years, Connie and Alex had talked about taking an evening sail, which would be their only opportunity with the summer demands of running *Lanterns*, but it had never worked out. Even this morning, they had needed to arrange with a friend to take on serving breakfast so they could get away for a few hours. They worked hard for six months, April through October, so they could travel and "play hard," according to Alex, for most of the remaining months.

A new vendor, *Spunks*, selling flavored pumpkin seeds in sleek black packaging, caught her eye, and Connie listened to his pitch, sampled the Garlic Pepper Kick, and bought a couple of bags.

She cut back across the street to the Freeland

glassblower's tent. Glass flowers and leaves on rebar stems glowed in the morning sunlight. A new addition this year was a rippled glass leaf in green and gold, which Connie knew would complement the ones she already had in planters on their deck. During the winter she brought the glass art pieces inside and decorated them in white lights to brighten shadowy corners.

Forkedelic.com, Fun Art Jewelry From Your Dining Table, was next. This craftsman from California will create rings, necklaces, and pendants from your silver cutlery. Connie admired how the fork tines were used in the designs as well as the ornate handles.

When Connie reached the wharf corner of Alexander Street, she paused to take in the scene before starting along Front Street, where oil/watercolor paintings, fabric creations, intricate baskets, candles, and pottery/ceramics were all artfully displayed. Waiting at the junction with Main Street would be *Knead and Feed's* table of generous cinnamon rolls, thick and springy, with just the right amount of icing.

Festival-goers of all ages in upbeat spirits made their way among the tents. Connie took in the hum of conversation, greetings, and comments around her. The crowds were building and she wondered as she did every year why people brought their dogs. Yes, they were leashed – even some with muzzles – but they had to weave through a throng of legs, eye-to-eye with the stroller set. Water stations were set out, but dogs were still panting and wary in the rising temperature. The only dog that seemed to be enjoying the event was a long-haired dachshund in a small blue cart with a parasol attached for shade, a bumper sticker on the back of the cart claiming, "It's all about me!"

After climbing a block up the North Main Street hill she turned right onto Coveland again at the *Bayside Kites* tent. Kites of all sizes and colors fluttering in the breeze off Penn Cove always anchored this entry corner. She crossed the street to some of her traditional favorites: *Whidbey Island Fudge Company*, for an orange chocolate sample; *Holmquist Hazelnut Orchards*, from Lynden; and *Just Toffee*, specialty foods that made welcome gifts.

Halfway along Coveland, she stepped into the *Bayside Treasures* tents, which held hundreds of hand-crafted home-décor signs and garden art. Bursts of laughter at the signs were contagious as people read them aloud.

WELCOME TO OUR HOT TUB.
WE DON'T SKINNY DIP. WE CHUNKY DUNK.

The Rustic Garden featured metal garden art, and Connie spied life-sized metal quail families. Along with her colorful selection of glass art she decided to start a metal collection with a single quail and add a quail each year. She and Alex enjoyed watching the families of live quail with chicks scurrying through their yard.

She was almost back at the post office after picking up her glass art leaf, ready to sit down and relax, thinking she'd give Alex a call, when she saw that he was already there, parked in another "10 minutes only" space.

"Hey, Con, that was good timing. I just used up

my ten minutes to run down to the wharf and pick up tickets for this evening's sail on the *Lady Washington*."

"Oh, Alex, way to go!" They stowed Connie's festival finds in the trunk and she gave him a hug.

"There are days when I definitely think I'll keep you. It's a perfect chance to be out on the cove; after a day like today there'll be a fiery sunset over our island for sure."

ANGELS WE HAVE HEARD...

"Crap!" mutters the Christmas angel as her cowboy-booted toe catches the hem of her long, wind-whipped gown, sending her careening into her companion. Angel One recovers her balance, bending her head to the task of righting her halo atop long blond hair.

"Watch where you're going," snaps Angel Two as she raises her own gown to clear a furrow, exposing striped leg-warmers.

"We're already supposed to be at the manger," whines the third angel, adjusting Angel One's tilted wings. "I can't believe I said I'd do this." The angel trio trudges on across the rough field under the starry brilliance of a Christmas Eve sky.

The Christmas pageant begins; stillness settles over the crowd ringed around sets of the outdoor Nativity scene in this South Texas climate so similar to that of Bethlehem.

Chapel teens organize this three-part drama that plays each Christmas Eve, taking the roles, acquiring an infant, and persuading local farmers to provide friendly animals.

In the first scene, Joseph and Mary are still at home in Nazareth contemplating their trip to Bethlehem. Joseph assists Mary onto the back of a rambunctious little donkey, and they fast-forward in time to the second scene, the Inn-keeper's entrance, where accommodation in the stable is arranged.

Sandra McGillivray Ortgies | 39

The manger set is in darkness. Sheep, calves, and nonrecruited squirrels are all in position. "Baby Jesus," in his Texan dad's arms, is waiting in the wings while the rest of the cast, in varying degrees of readiness, step into roles and places.

The angels glide in behind Mary after initially flirting with shepherds and Wise Men along the way. Something is happening here, a shift in angel attitude? We now have a trio of Christmas-card angels, silent and sweetly serene as they gaze at the star high on the Spanish-style chapel wall. Mary sits beside the manger and is handed the baby while Joseph leads the donkey to join the other animals.

All is calm, all is suddenly bright as the main spotlight sweeps the traditional scene. Families draw closer together as we sing "O Little Town of Bethlehem"; the busyness of our holiday preparations and Christmas Day plans seems forgotten in this moment.

This young Mary, much the same age as the mother of Jesus when he was born, cradles her borrowed baby, pulling her cloak more tightly around him while Joseph stands close by, slipping treats to sheep and calves.

This is what it's all about, as close an enactment as we can have; and the wonder of this gift encircles us all...especially the angels.

BEN AND FRANKIE

"What would Frankie do?" Ben threw a blanket over his shoulders and carried his first mug of coffee out to the deck in the early morning coolness. He wasn't sleeping worth a damn: couple of hours at the most, hadn't for a long time. He eased into Frankie's blue-and-white-striped chair, one of a pair, handcrafted in the Adirondack style; that way he didn't have to look at it empty. He placed the coffee mug on the yellow wooden cube that had held countless drinks and snacks while they had watched blowout sunsets together. Lifting Rudi up into the partner chair Ben shifted his blanket to share an edge. The dachshund was a good listener, but they'd both usually doze off again in the morning quiet.

It was becoming clear to Ben that the single neighbor women who lived on either side of his house – "Ditz and Dumpling," as Frankie had always referred to them – looked to him to take the lead in trying to resolve this bluff mess. A developer had somehow manipulated his way to gaining a permit to build on the cliff in front of them, land that had always been considered unsafe. The main issue for the three neighbors, though, was the fact that their view of Puget Sound would be history once the building began.

The truth was that Frankie had handled any confrontations that cropped up, directly and with a certain measure of glee. She'd ramp up sixties rock-

and-roll, or music from *Mama Mia!* and dance around the house until she had a particular problem sorted out. Whirling by to "Dancing Queen," she would grab Ben by the shoulders. "We've got to get on this, Bugman," and proceed to smack down or smooth out any glitches in their lives. So, what the hell should he do now, start dancing?

Frankie was a writer, and "writers are nosy...in a good way," she'd say. Frankie had talked easily to strangers, interviews being her forte. She gathered information no one else seemed to have, attended community meetings, and wrote "zinger" letters.

The marriage they reveled in had abruptly ended six months earlier on a foggy morning on West Beach Road when Frankie's Mini Cooper was T-boned by a Humvee.

"Listen up, Benjamin. I need to talk to you."

Frankie had dropped in on his dreams before. Ben would wake up reaching for her with an urgency that had him almost falling out of bed.

But Frankie using "Benjamin" was not a good sign. Going all the way back to their university days when he'd studied entomology, she'd called him "Bugs" or "Bugman." She'd tongue-tripped over their wedding vows, repeating the unfamiliar "Benjamin," which was thereafter reserved for their occasional verbal set-to's.

Ben would use Frankie's given name only when making a point, and at some risk. Her parents had called her "Frangelica" after overly imbibing in the almond liqueur, resulting in Frankie nine months later.

"Here's what I'm going to do. I'm sending you a

good woman. *I get it that our definitions of a good woman may vary somewhat, but she'll be at least as attractive as Ditz on a good day, at least as fine a cook as Dumpling when she's not pouring more wine into herself than the recipe. But get this: She'll also have some smarts. From my vantage point, widows are eventually OK. It's you widowers who are train wrecks."*

"Back off, Frankie! I'll decide when a new woman lands in my life." Images of Frankie's belongings: the flannel shirts she'd "liberated" from him that were still tossed over chairs in their bedroom, her rainbow of Crocs lined up by the back door, and notebooks full of writing ideas and media contacts, spread out all over her desk just as she'd left them, surged into Ben's mind. There wasn't room for another woman in his house, let alone any other part of his life.

"Parting thought, Bugman. You've got to shape up and get your life in gear again. So watch for her when you walk Rudi on the beach, browse the aisles at Prairie Market, join in on septic tank discussions at the Rec Hall... or any of the other exciting things you do these days. I can't stand it!"

Rudi was making running motions and giving out small yips in his sleep as Ben woke up. Was Frankie barging in on his dreams too? Ben stretched his lanky frame and reached over to set Rudi down on the deck.

OK. He'd focus on getting some action started and stop acting like a victim. He'd investigate the builder and the firm that produced the geology report, and get professional photos of the undercut bluff that was eroding more each year; possibly even get television news coverage. Ben knew he had to move quickly and he felt more alive at this sunrise moment than he had in months. He turned with a wave to the sky and, calling Rudi, headed toward the kitchen, a second cup of coffee, and Frankie's contact list.

A PLACE CALLED PAHRUMP

Henry and Not Henry stand motionless in the shore reeds of the seven-acre lake at the end of an avenue of date palms. The resident herons are riveted on catching their next meal. It is a lesson in patience. The month of April that we spend at Lakeside RV resort in Pahrump, Nevada, each year holds all kinds of these moments to slow down and appreciate.

Pahrump, which is Paiute for "springs emerging from rock," is located sixty miles west of Las Vegas in the Pahrump Valley on the west side of the Spring Mountains. "Over the hump to Pahrump" is the common locale description. Ten miles farther west is the California border, and Death Valley is less than an hour's drive.

We've been coming to this 35-acre oasis sur-rounded by sage brush and tumbleweeds for over ten years. In April, the temperatures mostly stay between 75 and 80 degrees under blue, blue skies. Aquifer water irrigates the park, resulting in green grass, pines, and willows thriving alongside palms and desert flowers. Roses in clay pots from the local nursery edge our patio. Roses do well in the desert, given enough water. They ride home to Whidbey Island, Washington, with us in the back seat of the pickup, acclimating along the way.

Individual touches appear among the various recreational vehicles: imaginative yard art, wine signs, and outdoor décor. The spare tire cover on a Jeep tow car states, "I Goes Where Ize Towed, I Hope." Motorhomes with clustered strings of lights underneath them appear to be perched on nests of white Christmas lights at night. Portable fire pits and container plants abound. Awnings and carpets make patios into outdoor living rooms; perfect weather helps. And in the soft desert evenings, the sound of banjo music carries across the lake.

There is ample space between the 55-foot-long sites, and every year we settle into the same spot beside the lake in our 26-foot Arctic Fox Trailer, behind the small onsite casino, sort of our *Cheers* in the desert. The casino staff hails from all over the country, and we can pick up on various accents when the bar servers come through calling out "Cocktails!" Some come to the desert planning to make enough money to move on, and then end up staying to make Pahrump their home. They visit with the regulars and with us short-timers. Music from the sixties and seventies, sometimes live, competes with the sounds of the slots action. A couple of hours of nickel gambling with a twenty-dollar stake is fun and once in a while, profitable.

Desert mornings are the best. Mauve shadows lie gently in the mountain crevices as we walk laps around the lake. Five laps, about two miles, is how I start each day. Newly hatched ducklings are often out in mini-armadas with their parent ducks. We try not to get too attached to these little charmers that visit the site and stand on our feet. They usually have a short life, as the lake is stocked with bass that torpedo up to the surface and swallow a duckling whole. This can cause hysterics in some of the RVers and a little heartache in others. There'll be fifteen ducklings one day, nine the next, and so it goes.

No picturesque town square graces Pahrump, and first-time visitors do try to find one. Highway 160 is a "just grew" strip of billboards and jumbled businesses: casinos, permanent fireworks stores, fast-food chains, and gas stations. The big boxes, Walmart and Home Depot, have appeared in the last few years. But up in the hills is Pahrump Valley Winery that wins national wine awards and houses an upscale restaurant that requests "reasonable casual" as its dress code. Landscaping is centered on the vineyard that features an area for concerts. It is one of the pretty parts. Mountain Falls Golf Club with a waterfall is another oasis, and Lakeside RV Park is the third. The RV park is three miles south of downtown, out the desolate Homestead Road, which moves us to warn first-time guests, "You'll think we have lost our minds, but wait until you get here."

The community library is a gem and we use it a lot. The library sponsors programs that bring members of the writing community together: Shakespeare Round Table, Play Writers Guild, Tumbleweed Tales Society for short stories and poetry, and Haikunami to inspire a tsunami of Haiku. Book signings with local authors are popular, as is the Favorite Author Book Club. This library was in place long before there was a hospital in Pahrump. The locals would comment that they could always go to the library and read up on what might be wrong with them.

Back at the park, we get into a pattern of doing

whatever suits the moment. The pool is large and not that busy, so we can actually swim laps. Canoes and kayaks are available on the lake shore and along with walking, we are getting plenty of outdoor exercise. We've been asked, "What is there to do in Pahrump?" We are quick to answer, "Not much, but that's the way we like it." Books, biking, and get-togethers with RVing friends from past years for an occasional potluck and cards round out our days at Lakeside.

Over the years, it has occurred to me that the park is a microcosm of people coming and going: a place for some of the best of times – like our Germany Gang Air Force reunion this spring – and for one of the worst. A memorial by the lakeside path honors Deputy Ian Deutch, who was gunned down in the casino parking lot responding to a domestic dispute only weeks after returning from Afghanistan. The Pahrump community came together at the park amphitheater at twilight – hundreds of people, locals and visitors, surrounded by the dusky mountains and starry desert sky.

We did April in Paris when we were stationed in Germany; April in Pahrump is what we do now. We arrive from the Pacific Northwest each spring yearning for the bone-warming sunshine and outdoor leisure living. How ready we are to ease back into this community of contrasts where we take the time to savor each day.

Coming over the "hump" from Las Vegas at night, we are always surprised at the sprawl of lights from one end of the valley to the other. Pahrump really looks like something at night. Pahrump always feels like everything our chosen getaway place should be.

RIDING THE RIM

Sparkling spring sunshine and smells of sodden
    earth
Green buds and moss-lined crevices soften shiny
    cliffs
Early March on the California coast, riding the rim
    of Redwood National Park
Crescent City behind us when an orange barricade
    straddles our lane

Okay with highway delays, we read and stretch and
    chat with flaggers
Miles of Oregon coast roadwork yesterday, seasonal
    storms on a worn-out surface
Pavement slippage and seeping slides reduce parts
    of Highway 101 to one lane
The where of this California delay has my attention,
    waiting on the edge of what-if

Giant Redwood down across the highway
Its fan of roots reaching skyward on the high side
Star top over the ocean side where we can hear
    Pacific surf hundreds of feet below
Ancient sisters hover, like witnesses to a fatal
    accident shocked and sad and silent

How many rings, old tree? No chain-saw bears for
    you
Wood artisans will fashion sturdy tables
Generations will gather, nourished with food,
    heartened by stories
At carved planks of redwood honoring a tree,
    celebrating a family

Carol Carnahan

CAROL CARNAHAN *has the incredible luck to live on*
Whidbey Island next to a Rhody farm. She has two pieces in an
anthology about a Nature Conservancy Preserve titled
Zumwalt: Writings from the Prairie, *and an article in*
Mushing Magazine, *"Can Sled Dogs Help Cure Cancer?"*
She was a winner in a Seattle Times writing contest called
Misadventures in Travel.

HOW TO BUILD A HUT

Consider first how slight a shelter is absolutely
necessary. – HENRY DAVID THOREAU

I cried when eight of our big cedars blew down in a windstorm. But a few years later the dried out branches were a fire hazard, and I started making arrangements to sell them to a mill. We were measuring them when Tom came up with his idea.

"Carol, we've had this Whidbey Island property for almost twenty years now. We come here and visit it, but we've never made it a home. Why not use these cedars? I have the skills and you have the money, honey, from the sale of your Alaska cabin. We both have the time. These are second-growth cedars, far too rare and beautiful to sell to the mill."

"But Tom, a lot more goes into a house than just the lumber. My little cabin didn't sell for enough to build a whole house, with plumbing and everything."

"OK, tell you what," Tom continued. "We'll build a tiny cabin on the property and live in it while the lumber from the cedar cures. We can put a lot of money aside that way."

It was tempting. Tom's love for working with wood and my penchant for cabins were practically shaking hands on the deal.

The tiny cabin was actually more compelling to me than an eventual cedar house. I had a cabin once. I chopped wood, hauled water, skied to class at the University of Alaska, and had no bills, except for taxes and electricity. After I left Alaska, I kept it for twenty-six more years, until Tom and I arrived one summer to find it tilting from permafrost melt due to global warming. I sold it to someone who promised to spend the money to save it.

We took our sandwiches over to the bluff and sat down on a fallen log. It was the last week of April, and sunlight was drifting in and out of a diaphanous cloud cover. The Olympic Range was out directly across Admiralty Inlet. Far away, the skyscrapers of Seattle looked tiny, not a part of this island world.

A container ship floated by, its deck cargo of red, grey, and blue containers gracing the waterway like a patchwork quilt.

A tugboat and barge passed, then a sleek black

half-submerged nuclear submarine, somewhat reminiscent of a cobra.

The land was in its young spring chartreuse. The maples still had the coral-colored stems that would be gone when the spring growth hardened up. For now it was beautiful – coral and pale green. Soft. Vulnerable looking. The wild coltsfoot flowers were out with their fluffy elongated feather-dusterlike blooms, trying to gain some territory over the stinging nettles.

We found a site with a view on all four sides, but protected from the constant onshore wind. I was easy to convince. To my way of thinking, this cabin would be my beloved Alaska cabin reincarnating itself.

Just like that, it was decided. We had the cedars cut to length and trucked to the portable sawmill of a meticulous ninety-year-old sawyer, who got more lumber from them than any computerized sawmill could accomplish. Trucked back to the property and ricked up to cure, the beautiful cedars were now 20-foot-long clear cedar boards.

There were constraints. We designed the cabin to be 10 feet by 12 feet. It had to be 120 square feet or less or the county would require not only a building permit but a septic system costing fifteen thousand dollars. We owned a share in a four-household well, but couldn't hook up to it without the septic system. So the parameters were no water, no plumbing, no driveway to the site to trample the meadow. We would have to wheel-barrow the materials in but it wasn't far. Electricity was a major expense – and hassle: the only permit or inspection required. But we needed it for reading lights and space-conserving electric baseboard heat.

We'd restored a sailboat together in the past, so we knew that we turned into workaholics when embarked on a project, especially Tom. So before we started the actual work, we gave ourselves a short vacation – a road trip, of course.

Highway 20, a major north-south route on the island, begins in Port Townsend across Admiralty Inlet from Whidbey Island. But no one we spoke to knew where it ended.

We caught Highway 20 after it crossed to the Whidbey side, presumably not on the ferry, though the road signs showed it that way. We followed it up the coast as it traced tidelands to the northern end of the island. Here it left salt water, turned east, and traversed the tulip fields and dairy farms in the Skagit Flats to the city of Mount Vernon. There it joined the Skagit River – second-largest river on the West Coast – and accompanied it north for fifty miles, leaving the river, finally, to turn east and cross the North Cascade mountains.

We put up the tent in a campground where the North Cascades bottom out into Eastern Washington flatland. Our old camping stove wouldn't start, and the zipper broke on my sleeping bag, so we ate granola bars and slept hungry and cold. The rule is: You can't complain; a good road trip involves vicissitudes.

Leaving Twisp, the last town of any size, Highway 20 runs through cherry and apple orchard country for about forty miles until it ends in (care to guess?) OMAK, the town no one knows. There Highway 20 splits into two roads, neither of them named Highway 20. This seemed both disrespectful and unfair.

We took Highway 20 back and left it at the Port Townsend ferry. (At least it wouldn't have to wait in the long line.)

Now the work would begin. The problem was going to be melding Tom's consummate craftsmanship with my slap-dash eagerness to finish a task.

A friend dropped by, and hearing the dimensions and that there would be no bathtub, dishwasher, stove, sink, or wide-screen TV, protested, "You're not building a cabin; you're building a peasant's hut!" He was right, of course, and from that time forward, the cabin's name was The Hut.

The Hut took us the spring, summer, and fall to build, working nearly every day. But before we could work efficiently, we needed to create a workable camp. Tom must have been one of those kids who built telephones out of two cans and a string, and dissected radios for fun. He took a party-size coffeemaker from the thrift store and built a head-high platform for it. Then he added a showerhead where the water comes out of the spout, using a tin can with holes punched in it. To take a shower you just stand on a ladder, pour water into the coffeepot, plug it in, test it to see if it is too hot or too cold, stand under the coffeepot, pull the string, and have a nice woodland shower with a view.

If it was too cold for an outdoor shower, we could go to a nearby state park which kept its showers open the year around. Their water had iron in it that made my hair smell like a cast-iron skillet but was OK otherwise. For drinking and cooking water, we used the kindly neighbor's hose.

The state park was a little too far away for other bodily needs, so we had a Porta-Potty in our driveway. Someone else came every week and cleaned it, a service every housewife deserves.

We had an outdoor kitchen and cooked with an electric skillet, a camp stove, a microwave, and another large electric coffeepot for use as a water heater for dishes. The only problem was slugs. I won't elaborate except to say you must look carefully in every pot before use, and prepare to replace your microwave if you accidentally microwave a slug.

The hardest work on the whole job was digging the holes for the pressure-treated posts that support the building, and then leveling them. Joists and sills were installed and foam board secured between the joists for underfloor insulation. And then the plywood floor was laid.

The most expensive material was the six windows, but with them we could watch the sun circle The Hut by day, the moon by night. Only very small buildings can have sunlight in the center of every room.

The second biggest expense was for the backhoe operator, who dug the trench for the electric line. The job that took the longest was refilling the 150-foot-long, 2-foot-deep trench. With a shovel. I didn't want the backhoe compacting the meadow, and by doing it myself by hand I saved the cost of another backhoe trip, though the neighbors thought I was crazy. I liked the physicality of the work and the feeling that I was making a con-tribution to The Hut that Tom was essentially building all by himself

I also contributed by holding things down in the ever-present wind, doing nailing that wasn't going to show, and carrying things. My most important job was lost-tool finder. This hated job used up hours at a time, driving me crazy, and often culminated in a trip to the hardware store for a replacement anyway.

After the walls were framed and sheathed with plywood on the outside and fiberglass insulation on the inside, the ceiling framing went up, stuffed with insulation. Then a layer of plywood followed by a layer of roofing paper. We also stapled roofing paper on the outside of the walls. Finally we were ready for the green metal roof. It was tricky because it sloped steeply, the ladder wouldn't reach the peak, and the tops of the screws just barely stuck out enough to give purchase to our boots. It was sort of like rock-climbing, even including the belay. The wind caught the metal panels and tried to pull them away from us like kites. When we got the roof on, though, its forest-green surface echoed the conifers that surrounded it, and The Hut suddenly belonged in its setting.

Tom installed and trimmed the windows, and left for a business trip, leaving the shingling to me. I shingled the whole hut before he returned, enjoying being out from under his critical eye and watching the shingles cover the roofing paper row by row. The shingles – a product of the forest, not the factory – felt good under my hands.

Shingling is repetitive work and thereby meditative work. I thought about other people who love cabins: Annie Dillard wrote in *Teaching a Stone to Talk* that opening her summer cottage was like being born.

E.B. White, whose cabin was a boathouse, wrote in "Second Tree from the Corner": "Here in the boathouse I am a wilder, and it would appear, a healthier man, by a safe margin. I have a chair, a bench and a table and I can walk into the water if I tire of the land."

People who love cabins tend to imbue them with magical properties. Sequestered in our cabins and unsnarled from everyday life, we can believe that all our innate creativity will rise to the surface and make us whole. And who's to say it doesn't work, even if it occurs as a self-fulfilling prophecy.

Tom came back, complimented my shingle work, strung wiring, and installed some light fixtures; and suddenly the outside of The Hut was finished!

As the trees began dressing themselves for fall, we started on the last major job: installing tongue-and-groove knotty pine over every inch of the walls and ceiling. This took two of us: one to lower the next board into the groove, the other to bang it into place with a mallet.

We began on walls and ceiling surfaced with the exterior foil on the fiberglass insulation sheets.

Overlaying this with pine suddenly made The Hut into a minor work of art – like a wooden sea kayak.

Now we could sleep in the high loft bed. We didn't mind being awakened by foghorns and the hooting of the Great Horned Owl. We awoke in the mornings to the misty light characteristic of islands.

Fall was advancing on us, but we still had work to do, and we were getting tired and cranky. We decided we needed some time apart, and scheduled individual excursions every few days. One of us could bicycle to the post office to get the mail and put the bike on the bus's bike rack for a free ride home while the other visited the library. The state park had miles of trails: trails through old-growth forest saved from logging years ago by citizen activists, a trail to a world-class giant cedar, flat trails, trails with elevation gain, beach trails, brushy trails, and quagmires.

I rode my bike to the park on a day when it was my turn to escape. The tide was out. Little mounds of sand with pencil-diameter holes in their centers marked clams in hiding. People had built beach bowers of driftwood big enough to lie down in and take a nap.

The clear weather ringed me with mountains: the Olympics to the west, some jagged peaks in Canada to the north, and the enormous white dome of Mt. Rainier to the south. The Cascades are not visible from this side of the island, but I knew they were there, completing the circle of peaks created by the Ice Age.

A heron fished just offshore. A dog ran down

the beach, spotted me, and ran back the way he came. Wait a minute! It wasn't a dog, but a long-legged coyote out in broad daylight for some reason of his own.

When I was ready to leave, I found I had forgotten the combination to my bicycle lock. I had to walk home.

We officially moved to the island in late fall. We rented a U-Haul and started loading. The hardest thing to load was our green sofa. We decided I should drag it down the sidewalk while Tom backed the truck up to the sidewalk. So I was pulling the sofa by its arm with my back to the road when I heard a back-up signal. You know – *ding! ding! ding!* But I was so used to that signal from the garbage trucks that it didn't register. Next thing I knew, Tom had backed into me with the U-Haul truck. Luckily I was catapulted onto the sofa, and Tom felt intuitively that he had hit something and stopped. I escaped with only a bruised tailbone – a literal stroke of luck.

Then as we were driving down the freeway, people kept waving, pointing, mouthing words, and making faces at us. We assumed they were having road rage because we were driving below the speed limit. Eventually, however, some intuition prompted Tom to pull over. We were shocked to find that the U-Haul's big doors had come open, and the 10-foot-long loading ramp had sprung out and was trailing the truck like a tail. We were very lucky that we did not get a $250 ticket or kill someone.

The next stage of the trip involved taking the car ferry to Whidbey Island. We drove on board, following the deckhand's directions. Suddenly the U-Haul came to a sudden stop and the deckhand's face went white. We had driven the right side of the truck under the metal beam supporting the upper car deck, which wasn't quite as high as a U-Haul truck. Have you ever noticed that U-Haul trucks have heavy pieces of steel along the top of the cab? We had only the fifteen-minute crossing time to get unstuck from the beam. What to do?

Tom freed us from the beam by letting most of the air out of the right-side tires. We limped lopsidedly off. No damage to either the truck or the ferry. The captain only had to delay the return trip for a few minutes.

We settled into our tiny 10-by-12-foot cabin on the island and tried to normalize our lives. We were getting by with this lifestyle, saving lots of money, and even starting to feel a little proud of ourselves. But we did have a problem with cabin fever, living in such a small space.

As much as I revere Thoreau, I never intended to live with another person in a cabin 30-square-feet smaller than the cabin where Thoreau lived alone.

We were happy for the diversion when a rare snowfall sent us cross-country skiing at historic Fort Casey. We were skiing on the blufftop when we spotted the nuclear submarine coming in from the Strait of Juan de Fuca. It was very strange to be skiing and simultaneously watching a nuclear submarine! The good part was that it was being towed by a Navy tug.

Snow continued to fall until we were

snowbound from the largest blizzard in Washington's recent history. Our Christmas dinner was going to be limited because we couldn't get out to shop, but the power was still on, so we had heat and a radio.

We were warm and snug for Christmas in our cozy little cabin. I practiced "Amazing Grace" on my old accordion. Tom played "I Just Go Nuts at Christmas" over and over on his mandolin.

But we didn't go nuts that year, though it was an option I certainly considered. Sequestered in the tiny cabin in the forest while the snow piled up, we were backed right up against elemental truths. And you know what, my friends? Life was good.

Bill of Materials: 6-by-6 treated lumber for posts, concrete, gravel (for post holes), 2-by-2's, 2-by-4's, 2-by-6's, 4-by-8's, framing nails (sinkers), finish paneling, shingle nails, metal roofing screws, other nails and screws, plastic for vapor barrier, ½-inch CDX (plywood) for sheathing, ¾-inch plywood for floor, hurricane ties (rafter top plate), roofing felt, foam board, fiberglass insulation, metal roofing, flashing, caulk, shingles, windows, one French door, tongue-and-groove pine, electrical panel, breakers, Romex, outlet boxes, switches, outlets, electric baseboard heaters, light fixtures, door-lock hardware.

The cabin cost about $5,000 for materials, plus another $2,500 for everything needed to have electricity.

Rowena Williamson

ROWENA WILLIAMSON *wrote her first book at age ten. It was, of course, about a horse. Moving forward, she turned to art, then back to writing. Two of her historical novels,* Escape to the Highlands *and* MacGregor's Bargain, *won awards at Pacific Northwest Writers Conference. She also wrote two historical romances,* Ryan and the Redhead *and* Ryan and the Redhead and The White Hag, *and is currently working on a short story and a sequel to* Escape to the Highlands. *Rowena lives in Coupeville with her Scottish Deerhounds, Taz and Ryan, who show up occasionally in her novels.*

ISLAND FEVER

An island has boundaries. People who live on Whidbey Island sometimes talk about "Going to America." Some find this desirable. Others see it as claustrophobic, and need to get away once in a while.

Anna saw it as a bit of both. Her husband Glen was content to spend all his time on the island with his various friends, fishing, playing poker at the lodge. But Anna's friend Grace was always happy to go anywhere, any time.

Today they took the ferry to Port Townsend. The ride across always gave Anna a sense of adventure. Sometimes, when the weather was wild, the ferry pitched and tossed, and tourists would stumble around grinning at each other. On another day in summer it would be warm enough to sit outside watching sailboats and fishing boats sprinkled across the blue water.

Today, when spring was slipping into summer, they planned to wander through bookstores, look into shops, discuss which restaurant would be perfect on such a sunny day.

The clustered buildings of Port Townsend came closer, mansions on the bluffs looming above the lower town, and the ferry slowed. The two women made their way down the stairs to stand near the bow, ready to get off as soon as the hawser was pulled back.

"Where shall we go first?" Grace asked.

Anna looked at her watch. "It's only ten. I have a few things to get here, but it's best not to have to carry things until we're nearly ready to go home."

Grace nodded. "Good idea. How about starting with a latte and taking it from there?"

They usually did begin this way: ordering their lattes and sitting by the restaurant window, watching boats and birds, and talking about their week, their husbands, their grandchildren. It was comfortable. The view from the café took in part of Whidbey Island, and Anna wondered idly what Glen was doing. She hoped he remembered to let the dog out before he went off somewhere.

"Oh! I remember something I have to pick up. Glen's birthday is next week, and I want to go to that nice men's store and get him a shirt or two." She shook her head fondly. "You know how they are, wearing the same shirt till it's a rag."

"Oh, yes, they are creatures of habit." Grace finished her latte and added brightly, "Well, shall we get to work?"

Bright sun and a little breeze gave Anna the feeling that this would be a perfect day. She would find two shirts for Glen, maybe something for herself in that great little consignment store around the corner.

As they walked down Water Street, she looked up at the bluff looming above the downtown shops. A steep stairway led to houses above. The big red storm-warning bell stood halfway up.

"Come on. Don't you want to shop before lunch?"

Anna turned and smiled at her friend. "I certainly do. I'll get those shirts right now, and then let's go to the consignment shop. After that the only plan I have is to spend at least an hour having a great lunch where we can look out toward Whidbey."

She halted for a moment and looked back at the bell tower and the cozy cafes at the foot of the slope. Grace asked, "What's the matter? I thought you were in a hurry."

"Weird. For a second I thought I heard the thing ring."

"Hah! You're probably wine-deprived. Let's get

the stuff bought, and eat!"

The shirts were easy. In less than half an hour Anna had searched, examined, and chosen two shirts and paid for them; and they were on their way to the consignment shop.

"How about this, for the next party?" Grace held up a slinky black dress. "It's got maybe a yard of fabric."

"Oh, nice. You know, I'm really not in the mood right now. Let's go eat. You pick."

"No contest. I want to try that place in the old hotel. You know, the one Liz told us about, on the water side."

"I'm good with that."

As they left the consignment shop, Anna turned and looked back at the fire alarm tower. Something…

"Come on. I hear they have all sorts of killer drinks."

"I thought we were going for the food."

"Well, that too. It's so warm now, and the breeze has died down. It'll be nice to sit outside."

They climbed the stairs to the top story of the hotel and found an empty table on the deck. A waiter appeared with a wine list and two menus which seemed to have something for every taste.

"This will take a while, but I know what wine I want," Grace said. "This is definitely a white wine sort of day."

The waiter took their wine orders and disappeared, and they began to study their menus.

"Good grief, I'll never make up my mind!" Grace looked over her menu at her friend. "What's the matter?"

"I don't know. I just felt funny for a moment. You know, kind of dizzy."

"Well, I don't wonder. You don't eat enough. You're probably really hungry. Am I right?"

"Uh-huh, I guess." Anna managed a weak smile. "If I didn't know it was impossible, I'd swear I have morning sickness." She drew a deep breath and began to examine her menu.

"Well, I'm having a hamburger and fries. I'm in the mood for simple food. And I'll have a dessert – just can't make up my mind which one."

When the waiter appeared with the wine, Grace ordered a rare burger and Anna, still wondering about her nausea, ordered pasta.

"Feeling better now?" Grace asked after they had tasted their wine.

"Yeah. I'll be fine." Anna tried to think of something that would divert Grace's attention. "Um. How are the grandkids doing?"

Grace beamed. "Oh, they're all great. Angus is on the football team. Lilian is graduating and going to UCLA… My God, Anna, you're white as a sheet! Sit back down!"

"No. We have to leave now!" Anna had suddenly remembered the last time she had felt this way. "Grace, trust me. I felt this nausea when I was in the Loma Prieta quake in California. We're going to walk past the waiter, and I'm going to tell him to start looking for a way to get the people out."

Grace stood, looking doubtful, but as Anna put some bills on the table and walked toward the waiter, she followed.

Anna approached the waiter and spoke softly. "Please believe me. There's going to be an earthquake in minutes. I've left enough money at our table to cover our lunches, so I'm not trying to get away without paying. Just start clearing people. My friend and I are going down now, unless you believe me and want me to help."

The waiter backed away, eyeing her, looked across and saw the bills on the table, and nodded. "I'll tell the boss. We've been trained for this. I just hope you're wrong."

Relieved that the waiter seemed to take her seriously, Anna led the way down the stairs.

"I still don't know how you know an earthquake's coming…"

The staircase rocked slightly, and they heard a crash in a closed room next to the stairs. The two women looked at each other and ran down to the street door and out to the curb. Grace stopped to look back at the building, and Anna grabbed her hand and pulled her out into the street.

"Don't stop!" she yelled, just as the pavement under their feet began rocking, nearly throwing them to the ground.

She looked around, trying to figure out the safest place, and decided it was better to sit right in the middle of the street. At least it would be if the ground didn't open up. She pulled Grace down with her and sat, pulling her jacket over her head.

"Cover your head and curl up!" Anna yelled above the sounds of falling debris. She looked up at the fire alarm tower on the crumbling bluff, watching it as it slid, then tipped, clanging, rolling into one of the cafés at the foot of the slope.

At the next rolling tremor, Grace screamed and Anna jumped, startled.

"What is it? Are you hurt?" Then, looking closely at Grace, she realized that her friend was hysterical. Anna pulled Grace around and held her face, staring into her eyes.

"You're all right. Nothing will hurt you." Anna tried to keep her voice steady. "We'll sit right here and wait for it to be over."

They heard a loud rumbling, and another jolt shook the ground. Anna sent a silent prayer that Glen was safe on Whidbey. She pulled out her cellphone. No bars. All around them the sounds of alarms from cars and buildings filled the air. She turned to look at the building they had lunched in. It swayed, and shingles fell to the ground. *Oh, please don't let it fall this way.* She felt that any minute she would give way to panic, shove Grace away, and run wildly toward the boat harbor.

A momentary stillness of the earth. Around them, the sounds of crashing wood, alarms, screams… People ran past them and parked cars bounced onto sidewalks. Creaking sounds came from the swaying old buildings. Then it seemed that all sound stopped, except for the alarms.

Grace pulled back from Anna's arms, her face stricken. "Is it over?"

"Probably not. There will be aftershocks. But we're OK." *For now…*

She stood up and pulled Grace to her feet and brushed some of the dust off her.

People had begun to wander around looking dazed: a young woman comforting her baby, and elderly man being helped by a teenager. Suddenly part of the facade of the building where they'd lunched began to lean forward.

"You're not hurt anywhere, are you, Grace?"

Her friend shook her head, tears still rolling down her cheeks. "What about Whidbey Island? Our husbands? They will be so worried..."

If they're still alive. No, I can't think about that.

There was still the sound of breaking glass and falling wood, but more people began coming out from wherever they had found safety. Some of them were pulling out cellphones, but Anna was sure they wouldn't work.

The local police were gathering, and Anna heard sirens coming. The tall red fire alarm tower lay on its side, its top stuck through the window of the bistro. Somewhere someone was screaming, and Grace winced and covered her ears. They watched two officers running toward the sound. Anna took Grace's hand and walked toward the group of firemen who had just appeared.

"Is there anything we can do?" Anna asked the closest one.

"Are you a nurse?"

She shook her head. "No. I was a teacher in the Bay Area, so I've had some emergency training for earthquakes."

He examined her, and she knew he was

thinking: "She's too old for much."

"Has there been local training here? Aid stations?"

"Yeah. There are ones being set up down around the ferry dock, down at the town hall, and another up on the hill."

She thanked him and turned to Grace. "Let's go down there and see if we can help."

Grace sighed, and her voice quavered. "I just want to know that Bob's all right. Aren't you worried about Glen?"

"Of course I am," Anna snapped, and then felt guilty as she saw her friend's woebegone face. "But if we're helping here, it'll take our minds off our worries."

Grace took a deep breath. "Maybe they will know what's happening on Whidbey."

When they arrived at the town hall, an emergency station was being set up. A harried-looking woman in a Red Cross vest welcomed them.

"I'm Rose Moffat. I work here. Are you volunteers? You're not injured, are you?" She looked at Grace. "Why don't you go over and sit down for a while. In just a minute I'll bring you something to drink."

"I'm Anna Kent. I've had some training. Have you had any news from Whidbey Island?"

"No, but I heard those men in the corner saying they had seen smoke."

Anna sighed. "We live on Whidbey. Our husbands are there. Of course we're worried about them. But what can I do? Can I set up a field station?"

"I know where supplies are kept." Rose looked over at the men. "They're volunteers too, but let's just get on with it. People will be coming in soon. There's a soft-drink machine over there. Get your friend something with a lot of sugar."

As Anna pulled a soft drink out of the freezer, the emergency radio began to blast where the men stood.

"A 7.5 earthquake centered in the Strait of Juan de Fuca between Dungeness Spit and Victoria. Reports are coming from the Olympic Peninsula and Whidbey Island. Be prepared for more quakes, and keep people away from shores along the strait and Admiralty Inlet. Military personnel return to bases."

In the silence that fell after the report, Anna and Rose began setting up the station, and the men began bringing supplies up from the basement. The building shook, and something fell noisily. Anna looked across at Grace, who stared back at her. She motioned to her friend, and Grace dutifully stood and came to help.

"Do you think they're all right?" she whispered to Anna.

Another rumble, but this time nothing fell.

Anna was tempted to say something comforting, but she said simply, "I don't know. I do know we'll be here for a while, and we can hope they're safe and feel we are too. It'll take a little time to set up communications."

She looked up as people began filing in. "I do wish I hadn't wanted to escape from Whidbey." She gave an ironic grin. "We got our wish, didn't we?"

A
WHIDBEY ISLAND ROMANCE

"Whidbey Island has an odd shape, like some sort of creepy deep sea creature, with a little head and a great big belly, and a little tiny tail. And between the belly and the tail is little Camano Island."

Lara glared at her computer. Could a travel writer have writer's block? Who would want to go to a place with that description? She tried another passage.

"As the ferry leaves quaint Port Townsend on its journey to Whidbey Island, tourists flock to the railings in hopes of seeing Orca whales. They see men in small boats scattered across the blue water cast for salmon. In one boat a grinning fisherman stands, hands spread wide to show the size of his catch. The ferry passengers applaud."

Not bad. But where to go from here? She shut her eyes and sighed.

"The ferry dips into the wake of an outward-bound cargo ship and bounces up. Strangers grin at each other as they steady themselves. The bright sun and brilliant blue skies can be deceiving. Tourists dressed for summer shiver inside, sitting in front windows, watching Whidbey Island approaching, the lighthouse on the hill and campers on a narrow stretch of beach below." That was trite. She could

feel anxiety building at the thought of missing the deadline in ten days.

OK, what now? How could she stretch this out so it would be appealing? Pushing herself away from the computer, she stood, looking out over Penn Cove. On the eastern horizon, snow-covered Mt. Baker and the Cascade mountains stood out against a clear blue sky. Her deerhound looked up at her, tail thumping.

"No joy, Taz. You won't get fed if I don't write."

She wandered into the kitchen and pulled a bottle of wine from the refrigerator.

"It's five o'clock somewhere," she assured Taz as she poured a glass of Whidbey White. "And I really need this." What would happen if she couldn't make her deadlines? Walking out to the porch followed by Taz, she saw white sails drifting around the cliffs to the north. Her heart lifted as the *Lady Washington* appeared, heading for Coupeville on one of her rare visits. Lara sighed happily as more sails appeared. The *Hawaiian Chieftain*, sails catching an onshore breeze, swept past the smaller craft. Raising her glass to the ships, she watched them as they glided toward the dock, sails lowering as they neared it, to loud applause from people watching.

Taz stood and stretched and stared at Lara.

"OK, you win." Lara drank the last of the wine and stood up. "Want to take a walk?"

Taz perked her ears – or being a deerhound, the lower half of them – and her tail waved gracefully.

Leashed, Taz led her person along the sidewalk above the shore, investigating scents left by other canines as Lara brooded about the article she was supposed to be writing. A jogger swept by them and Taz tried to keep pace with him. He grinned over his shoulder at Lara.

"Cool pup," he said, then ran on.

She sighed, wishing he had stopped to talk. She loved living in Coupeville, but it wasn't a great place to meet single men. What was worse, her married friends kept looking for men for her. She sometimes felt like some sort of market item.

"Tell you what, Taz, let's go to the beach."

Taz half perked her ears. She knew "go."

There was a quiet beach on the west side where the hound could safely run, and the moment she was released she went to full speed, kicking up sand at each leap.

Lara watched her and trailed behind, looking for agates. She had found several over the time she had lived on Whidbey Island, and kept them in a glass dish on her coffee table. There was always something to see on the west beaches: cruise ships from Seattle on their way to Alaska, a ferry pounding its way from Port Townsend. One enchanted day she had watched a pod of Orcas making their way south.

Taz trotted back grinning, and leaned against her, ready now to walk beside her person. Lara bent to pick up the partial shell of a sea urchin. As always, the delicate sculpting of its interior design intrigued her. What part of the urchin's body went where?

When Lara first came to Whidbey Island three years ago, she had taken classes from Washington State University Beach Watchers. With the knowledge she gained, and deciding that she liked island life, she got a job with a national travel magazine. While the pay was sporadic, she managed with savings from her previous job at a dot-com company. If only she could think of something to write!

Now, at thirty-five, having found her perfect life (except for the looming deadline), she followed Taz down the beach, keeping an eye on the hound to make sure she didn't roll in something nasty. Bluffs rose to her right, crumbling reminders of the glacial age. The incoming tide began to creep up the sand and Lara whistled for Taz, who ignored her until Lara turned and walked back to the car; then she galloped back and sped past Lara, kicking up sand; then she turned, stopped, and panted, her tail wagging.

Lara shook her head as she opened the car's back door for her sandy dog.

"Thanks a lot, beast."

With the lowering sun, shadows begin to spread across fields of beets and cabbage and corn. Lara had written an article about the farmers on Whidbey Island who owned land purchased by their grandfathers in the nineteenth century. The road she drove on, the farms, the houses were part of Ebey's Landing National Historical Preserve.

OK, there was definitely another story there. Maybe on the latest generation, the emphasis on locally grown products, farmers market, college graduates who decided to return to the land. She nodded to herself as she pulled into her driveway. OK. That would work. Maybe.

After brushing the worst sand off Taz, Lara fed

her and sat at her computer. She looked at her watch. She had an hour before she met her friends. OK. She stared at the blank blue screen and sighed, then began.

"*The youngest generation of the original farmers on Whidbey Island are not following their ancestors, though they hold the same lands….*"

"That's awful." She scowled at the words, feeling a moment of panic.

"*Though they now have different methods, the youngest descendants of farmers who came to Whidbey Island are following the ancient rhythms of the land….*" Oh, how poetic. She pretended to gag.

She avoided looking at her calendar, and everything she wrote got worse. She looked at her watch. Thank God. It was time to meet her friends.

Changing her T-shirt for a cleaner one, putting on a jeans jacket to fend off the cooling breeze, she walked down the hill to the wine bar to meet Alice and Mare. It had become a Friday night tradition to have an appetizer, taste wines, then go to someone's house to watch a movie.

They got a table just before the place began to fill with crews from the tall ships.

"Oh, to be twenty again," Alice said as a suntanned crewman strode by. They giggled as they raised glasses to each other.

"How's the writing going? Got anything yet?" Mare asked.

"Uh-huh, I have an idea, but somehow the words aren't coming."

Lara leaned back looking around, waved to a

friend. One of the joys of living in Coupeville, she thought, was the friends she had made. She would hate to be forced to leave them. After their wine, they wandered through the twilight to Mare's house to watch their weekly movie; then Alice walked down the hill to her house, Lara up the hill to hers. Taz greeted her, then went back to lie on her bed.

Lara turned on her computer and stared at the blank blue screen. It stared back at her.

"The sturdy young descendants of Whidbey Island pioneers..." It was getting worse. Maybe mentioning a name. Lara had become friendly with Joan Logan, a 25-year-old who worked on her parents' farm. OK.

"Joan Logan came back to run her parents' farm after deciding she preferred Coupeville to Los Angeles." Dull dull dull.

Lara sighed and got up, wandered around her house and out to the porch, where faint sounds came up to her from Friday evening celebrants. Taz came out and leaned against her. Lara stroked her silky ears.

"Hey, pup, I'd better get some inspiration soon or we're doomed. I have no idea what's going on, but nothing seems right, you know? I'm a writer; I've always been a writer, of one type or another; and now nothing is working." She wiped her eyes and sniffed. "It's only eight o'clock but I'm done in. Let's go to bed. Maybe I'll get an idea tomorrow." Taz wagged her tail.

When she climbed into bed Lara picked up a book she had started, a romance novel; she might as well finish it.

Lara was asleep before nine.

She woke at eight as Taz put her cold nose on her face.

"Well, I did have a good night's sleep," she said as she pushed back her quilt.

Nothing had appeared to help her start writing, so she showered and dressed and took Taz to the off-leash park for a run. Maybe it would get her brain working.

There were only three cars parked outside the chainlink fence. As Lara and Taz walked through the chainlink gate, a tall woman waved from the small-dog area as her two pugs barked fiercely at Taz.

"Hi, Lara. I haven't seen you in a while."

"Yeah, Amy. I've missed coming out, and Taz has for sure. I still haven't written an article for *Traveller's Joys*, and I haven't gotten an idea in a month."

"Oh, I'm sorry. I wondered why you hadn't come to our readers group. Well, good luck!" her friend called as Lara and Taz began jogging into the woods.

Taz broke into a full run, then turned back to race around Lara before racing off again, joy in every leap. As Taz disappeared Lara heard a deep, loud bark and began running. Another bark and she ran faster, terrified she might hear howls that would mean Taz was being attacked.

Breathless, she rounded a corner in the woods and the playing field came into view. Taz was playing with the biggest Irish Wolfhound she had ever seen. Taz looked minute as she bounced around him. She turned and saw Lara and loped toward her, followed by her new playmate. Knowing it was better not to move as the two swept toward her, Lara watched them as they separated and ran past her.

"Conor!" The baritone roar stopped the hound. He pivoted and raced toward a man emerging from the trees.

Taz trotted to stand by Lara as the man and the hound approached them.

"I apologize if Conor frightened you. He was thrilled to find a playmate, especially such a beauty." He held out his hand. "I just found this park. I'm new to the island. Alex Morgan."

Lara shook her head. "I heard Conor's voice and thought of the Hound of the Baskervilles. Taz is no lightweight, but he sounded enormous. I'm Lara MacRae."

"A good name for a deerhound owner. Well, you know the big sighthounds: big marshmallows." He laughed. "I almost asked, 'Do you come here often?'"

"Often as I can. I live in Coupeville."

"I live outside Coupeville."

They both laughed, looked at the dogs, back at each other.

"Well, I'd better get on my way." Lara hooked the leash to Taz's collar.

"Yeah, me too. Um. If you're not doing anything, could we meet somewhere for a drink – if you drink."

"I'd like that. Do you know Front Street Grill? They have a happy hour."

"Sure. Four-thirty or so?"

He nodded and turned to leave, then turned back.

"Uh, if you're leaving too, mind if we walk back to our cars together?" She saw his eyes were as dark as his hair – a true black Celt.

"Well, we have to go to the only parking lot, so I guess that's reasonable."

"So, how long have you lived in this secret corner of the nation? And where exactly do you live?"

She laughed. "Very near Front Street. I have a fenced-in area for Taz, and Conor is welcome if you want to leave him sometime. See you at Front Street."

As she drove away, the article was forming. "Whidbey Island dog parks. Where strangers become friends."

Pat Kelley Brunjes

PAT KELLEY BRUNJES *is a retired Speech and English teacher, librarian, and school administrator. She has a doctorate in Educational Leadership: Curriculum and Instruction. Her poetry has won honors from the Willamette Writers Association, the Washington Poetry Association, and the Whidbey Island Writers Association. She taught students of all ages how to read literature aloud, and coached many students to honors in Speech and Debate. She has a book of poetry,* Poetry from the Desert Floor. *"The Forest Fire" is from* The Last Confession, *her novel in progress.*

THE FOREST FIRE

The fire burned in the tops of the trees, out from the road, but dangerously close. Maggie removed the food from her backpack and put some of it in her firefighter's coat pocket. She checked for the knife, small spade, and binoculars she had put in at the base camp. To Susan and Jason, the campers she had found on the side of the road, she said, "I'll leave the rest of the food here. You are welcome to eat a sandwich and a dessert, but please don't eat all the food. We don't know how long we will be here. I brought enough food for one person for three days. There are now three of us, maybe even six of us, so portion out your eating. There is plenty of water, so drink water if you think you're still hungry."

"Got it," they said in unison.

"Now this is important," Maggie continued. "I'm leaving the truck here so you can get out if the fire takes a bad turn and I can't get back to you. If the family drives out of the campground, go back to the base camp with them, and leave me the truck. Otherwise, wait right here."

"We'll do exactly as you say." Jason took Susan's hand, and she held on tight.

Maggie slung the lightened backpack over her shoulder and headed down the road at a trot toward the campground to find the family that Susan and Jason reported were still in the danger zone. She watched the change in vegetation. The closer she got to the campground, the more crowded the pine trees became. *Fodder for fire*, she thought. As she ran, she couldn't help thinking of Father Matthew. She found comfort in thinking he might be waiting for her back at the base camp. Comfort, and something else she had no right to feel.

In twenty minutes she was at the campground. No sign of flames, but the smoke was becoming thick. She saw a new truck, but no sign of the family.

"Anybody here?" she yelled. She faced east, looking for the creek and the flames that Susan and Jason said they could see from the campground. She could see neither fire nor a creek. She walked toward the Subaru and noted that the campfire was cold, as if it had not been used for at least twenty-four hours. *At least these people know how to take care of a campfire,* she thought.

"Hello, anybody here?" Maggie continued to walk east. She came out of a stand of trees and there was the creek, and on its far bank she could see small clusters of fire high in the trees. *Oh, my God,* she thought. *Where are these people?*

Maggie pulled out her walkie-talkie and pushed the base camp commander's button. Ted answered.

"I have good news and bad news," she said. "I am at the campground. There's a big truck sitting here and not a soul in sight. I've yelled, and no answer. The creek is only a couple of hundred feet from the campground. The fire is in the tops of the trees on the other side, about a half-mile out, so it has come in on floating embers. It won't be too much longer and the trees will be fully engulfed."

"No sign of people? That does seem odd."

"I'll walk around and yell for a bit longer, but I won't stay if I see the trees are about to become engulfed."

"Maggie, please take care. By the way, Father Matthew is here waiting for you." Ted clicked off. Maggie stood for an instant staring at the phone. Father Matthew was there. She would get through this.

Maggie began circling the campground, calling for anyone close enough to hear her. Suddenly two people appeared. The woman was crying and waving her hands. "Help us!" she shouted.

Maggie sprinted over to them. "What is the problem?"

"We've lost our son. He disappeared while we

were packing the car. We have been looking everywhere for him. I don't know what else to do." The woman sank to her knees, holding her head in her hands and sobbing.

"I'm Maggie. What are your names?" She knew people responded better if you called them by name.

The man answered. "We are the Pointers, Evan and Pamela. Our son is Jon. He is six. He just disappeared. We know that seems impossible, but that's what happened. We've looked everywhere for him. We've called and called."

"I don't know what to do," Pamela wailed.

Maggie took control. "This is what you are going to do. You are to get in your car and drive out. When you get almost to the road, you will find a couple standing by my truck. Please pick them up and take them out. Head back to the base camp."

Pamela screamed. "Are you out of your mind? We can't leave our son. He's all we have."

"You can and you will," Maggie commanded. She wasn't sure she really felt that way, but to find this boy she didn't need flailing parents. "I will search for the boy, and I can do it much easier and much faster by myself. I have a fire-retardant coat and a tent. I know how to survive." She left out the part about the unpredictable nature of wildfires. "Hopefully, I won't have to use either one. You understand: I will bring him out."

"What if he's dead?" Pamela was crying so hard she was sucking air. Evan tried to hold her, but she was not to be consoled. She stood and pulled away from him. "We didn't mean to lose him," she said, as if Maggie might think they had deliberately left him.

"What was he doing when you saw him last? Did you see him walk off? Do you think he went down to the creek?"

"We were taking down the tent," Evan said. "It takes two of us to take it down and fold it. During that time he walked off. When we realized he was gone, we finished packing and set out to look for him. That was probably less than twenty minutes ago. We have no idea where he went. I really don't want to leave."

"I understand that," Maggie said, "but — how do I say this kindly — you are a hindrance. I am dressed for fire; you are not. I know my way around forest fires; you do not. Please get in your car and get to safety. I will find him and bring him back."

"Do you promise? Even if he's dead, you won't leave him?" Pamela broke into wracking sobs.

Maggie promised, but she wondered if even she could handle the sight of a dead child. She waited until the Pointers had driven away before she shed the backpack and the heavy coat. They would only slow her down. Right now she needed speed more than she needed fire protection.

Maggie set out for the creek. It seemed a young child would want to play in water, throw stones and watch the ripple, but where would he have gone that the parents couldn't find him? Somewhere along the bank, she guessed.

The creek was about a hundred feet wide, like a small river, cold and fast. It was possible he had fallen in. The banks were lined with small rocks and low brush. Jon could easily have slipped into the frigid water. If so, they might not find him until the fire burned itself out; but she brushed that thought aside. She had to find him now or run the risk of the fire jumping the creek.

Maggie called Jon's name over and over. The walkie-talkie buzzed. It was Ted. "What's the latest, Maggie?"

"I sent the parents out. The mother didn't want to go, but I told her she wouldn't be able to help. They finally left. I asked them to pick up Jason and Susan on their way out. Jason knows to leave me the truck. They should be out in about forty-five minutes. I'm scanning the creek bed. There is fire in the tops of the trees on the other side, but not yet hot. I'll have to find him soon. If this fire jumps the creek, neither of us will get out."

"Call the instant you find him. I'll be on the outlook for the parents. Maggie, take care of yourself." For a moment Maggie thought Ted might even care about her survival.

She ran along the creek bank for about a quarter of a mile from the campsite when she saw them. He was on an island in the middle of the creek, happily throwing rocks. Dressed in shorts, a T-shirt, and sandals, he was oblivious of the fire. Standing beside him was a brown mare, her nose down next to his head. Maggie stopped and stared. How did they get there? Where did the mare come from? She yelled Jon's name. The two looked up at the sound of her voice.

"Jon, I'm Maggie. Looks like you're having fun. How did you get out into the middle of the creek, and who is your friend?"

Jon smiled. "I walked on rocks," he said, and pointed downstream. Maggie could see where rock and dirt formed a tiny peninsula into the creek. "This is Narnia. She walked across from the other bank."

"You sure are brave," Maggie said. "I'm going to come and get you. I will take you to your mom and dad."

"We can't leave Narnia behind," Jon said emphatically.

Maggie looked at the mare. She was shaggy even for a hot summer day, a sign that she had not been cared for in a long time. She appeared to be calm. There was no sign the horse would run or cause trouble.

"I named her for the books my dad likes to read to me. There is a horse in one of the books, but I can't remember the horse's name, so I just call her Narnia." He reached up and patted the horse's nose. The horse nickered and made no attempt to run. Maggie was unsure whether the fire had gentled her or she was a tamed horse that got stranded in the fire. There was no way she could tell if the horse was broken. Once they got back to the truck, she would try and handle the horse. *I don't dare put a child I don't know on a horse I don't know,* she thought. *This would be a lot easier if Jon could ride her out.*

"You like the *Chronicles of Narnia*?" Maggie asked. "Those were some of my favorite stories when I was young." It was Maggie's attempt to build trust with Jon, but his happy mood began to fail.

"How come my mom and dad didn't find me?

Are they gone? We can't leave Narnia behind. She will die in the fire." For the first time, Jon looked like he was going to cry. And he acknowledged the danger.

"Your mom and dad went back to the main road. They looked all over for you and couldn't find you. They asked me to look for you."

"Are you a forest ranger?" Jon asked. "I always wanted to meet Smokey the Bear. I don't like all the smoke, though. It hurts my eyes."

"Tell you what," Maggie said, "you and I and Narnia are going to walk out of here and find your mom and dad." She picked him up and waded back to the shore. The mare followed.

Once on the bank, Maggie took another look at the trees. The fire was still in their tops, but she knew that would change as soon as the wind came up. She had to get out of here now. She picked up Jon and raced back to the campground, grateful that the horse stayed with them. She found her coat and backpack where she'd left them.

"You and I are going to do something fun," she said. "We are going to run and walk out of here. I'm very concerned that we get back to my truck before the wind starts blowing. I'm going to hold your hand the entire way. Do you think you can do that?"

"Sure, Maggie. I won't be afraid." He grabbed her hand as if he would never let go.

"That's right, Bucko." Maggie grabbed the coat and the backpack. Sandwiches would have to wait until they were safely back to the truck.

Maggie looked at the mare. The horse waited

quietly to find out what would come next. She made no attempt to run. Maggie put her hand out and patted her side. "Good girl. You don't seem at all spooked." The mare just stood and looked at her. "All I can do for you right now is hope you follow us out. Once back at the truck, I'll figure out something."

Maggie ran and walked and ran and walked. Jon held on and never cried or whimpered. The mare jogged along behind. Maggie continually reminded Jon that he was a strong boy and thanked him for saving the horse and helping her get out of the fire. They sang songs. By the time they reached the truck, Jon was singing at the top of his lungs. Relieved, they ran the last hundred yards. The mare trotted after them, then stood and watched. "Hey, Jon. I have some sandwiches and brownies. Are you hungry?"

"I'm starved."

"Jon, I want to thank you for helping me."

"You're welcome, Maggie." Jon looked at her with big brown eyes, not really sure what he had done to help, but he smiled a big, wide grin. "Maggie, my eyes burn, and I know Narnia doesn't like the smoke."

"I know. The smoke is getting thick and heavy. Let's grab some grub and get out of here." She pulled two sandwiches out of the backpack. "All I have are two roast beef sandwiches. One for you and one for me. That OK? I have several apples. Shall we give one to Narnia?"

"Yes, Narnia should have some apple, but I don't like roast beef," Jon replied.

"Well, young man, it's that or you starve."

"I guess today I like roast beef sandwiches," he said. Maggie cut an apple in half and offered it palm up to the horse. Narnia took the apple and chewed. She was so gentle, Maggie assumed someone had raised her. *What am I going to do with this mare?* Maggie thought. *There is rope in the truck. I can tie her to the truck, but then I'll have to drive five miles per hour. Not a good prospect for survival.*

"Good boy. Get in and we'll get going." Maggie held the door for Jon and helped him climb into the truck. She attached his seatbelt, handed him a sandwich, and watched him wolf down the food. *I'll bet from now on he'll love roast beef.*

"What are we going to do with Narnia?" Jon asked.

"There's a rope in here somewhere. We'll tie her to the truck." She found the rope and approached the horse. The mare backed away when she saw the rope, the whites of her eyes showing fear. Maggie approached her slowly.

"Come on, old dear. I know you'd rather come with me than burn to death in the fire." Maggie put her arm over the horse's neck, and pulled the rope around. She tied a loop. The mare shook her head, but did not fight the rope. Maggie secured the other end of the rope to the tail gate, and climbed into the truck with Jon. She turned the key, and the engine turned over smoothly.

"Let's go, everybody. We have to get out of here."

WHIDBEY ISLAND

How many times have we walked these beaches
sought shells and fossils of a thousand years
smelled seaweed in the foam
watched fading sunlight silhouette lace images in
our minds

come walk with me in this broad expanse
touch dry grass, new flowers, old trees
listen to the cacophony of birds
play music in our heads

when rain comes, foreshadowed by dark clouds and
wind
when night brushes away the clouds to open up the
skies to all eternity
remember our love
curl yourself around me until our promise is
fulfilled

LOST LOVE

I remember our promises
Made at fifteen
Forever, we said
Oh, the silliness of youth
I still catch myself
Watching for your face in crowds
I thought I saw you once in San Francisco
In a bookstore
The image of your father
But it wasn't you
I still look

Larry Shafer

LARRY SHAFER *is a retired litigation lawyer and judge. He lives in Langley on Whidbey Island, Washington. His legal exploits include a successful suit in the early 1970's which prevented the razing of Seattle's Pike Place Market. In 1966-67, he researched, advocated, and later directed the first legal services program in the nation under the new War On Poverty law. The program has now expanded to cover the entire state of Washington.*

BEYOND PATHOS

Anonymous we wander
A strange city a discovered village
Crowds in train stations bus stations airports
We stroll meander wait in line
Sit at bars
Eat at cafés
    wine and coffee aperitifs sidewalk tables
    fragrant loaves of bread just removed from oven
    at corner bakery
And share and touch souls of others through their
eyes, beyond pathos
Near telepathy
By their clothes bow ties pink shirts stocking caps
    high heels sneakers hiking boots white socks
    nylons blouse to the neck blouse with cleavage

shorts long pants skirts and dresses T-shirts
«be happy»
The language of their bodies
Nod the head shake the head roll the eyes
Expressions by arms and hands legs and feet shrugs
of shoulders
A stumble over a woman's purse on the ground
frustration drops his cane
Light in the eyes with smiles reveal epiphanies
One sits alone melancholy
Another shares eureka with a friend
Handkerchief held to tears
Frightened he looks down she touches his arm
looks in his eyes her face is empathy
one raised eyebrow eyes wide and damp
half a smile head angled to side
Three women share euphoria energy and laughter
Mother teases small girl cries lost inspiration
One preaches Jesus a companion blasphemes

Warmth circulates through my body
I have reached the flame of others the shed of tears
the soft touch between women friends the joyful
laughter of three
elderly men a face demonstrates despair

A leaf on a small branch is moved by a breeze and
dances on my cheek
I turn to it and say a silent thank you

Dorothy Read

DOROTHY READ *loves to tell a story and even more, to write one. She has concentrated on short fiction, but expanded her interests with* End the Silence, *the full-length memoir of a woman who survived the Japanese occupation of the Dutch East Indies (now Indonesia) during WWII and the bloody revolution that followed. Read debuts as a poet in the new WWG anthology, and her short piece, "Semper Fi," was inspired by her husband's final struggle with advanced COPD. Whidbey has been "home" since 1978, where Read has both pursued her own writing and mentored the writing of others as a teacher and editor.*

DOTS AND DASHES

I'm clearly not a poet, but I write it just because
I love to hear the syllables make music with their
    sounds,
to place the accents where they'll make the iambs
    ebb and flow,
the steady meter carries me, pentameter be damned.

On the wave of iamb bliss I suddenly may find the
syllables have changed their course and trochee
    comes to mind.

Say it! Shout it! Write it! Name it! Who cares what it
    calls itself?
Trochee, Spondee, Hip Hop blast, words beat the
    drum. I rest my case.

∞

SEMPER FI

Palliative gave Curative a little shove and said,
"I'll take over now."

"Not so fast, Palli. I haven't given up, and
neither has he."

"Yes he has. Look at him. He's through. I'll just
keep him comfy in his beddy-bye until Terminative
shows up." Palliative knew her job and did it well.

"This one's different; he fought Terminative
back in 'Nam."

"Get real, Curative. He's not going to get well."

"Maybe not, but he's going to get better. Now
back off."

It was always like this between the Morphine
sisters. Hard to believe they came out of the same
bottle.

In Memoriam

Jeff

If Dee had known it was his last meal
she'd have laced it generously with chocolate syrup.
Cereal, it was – gruel, really – creamy wheat.
She made it soupy so the swallowing
was easier. He took it from a silver spoon,
held steady by her practiced hand. "It's in my
    contract,"
she would say when he apologized
for needing help. His fading eyes held hers,
the only way for him to hold her now.
"You are so beautiful," he said,
his voice a raspy whisper, but she heard and
smiled and gulped the loving words that
nourished her while strength bled out in weeping
fits he did not see. She didn't know that this
    would be
her last meal, too.

Linda

Probably she reckoned she would sit out on the sun
  porch
in the wicker chair again. Probably she
thought she'd read *Green Eggs and Ham*
to grandkids and would write the recipe for
mac and cheese which everybody wanted.
Probably she thought she'd finish up the quilt she'd
started for the newest grandchild, due in June.
She thought she'd see tomatoes blossom in her
  greenhouse and
she'd watch the fruit mature, along with lettuce,
  spinach –
all the lovely sprouts that would become the
  vegetables
her progeny pretended to reject, but always ate.
She served up wisdom, too, on everything from
how long one should roast a goose to how one
deals with a cheating spouse. Probably she knew
how much they'd miss her wisdom someday
when she wasn't with them anymore.

 # Miko Johnston

Miko Johnston

MIKO JOHNSTON, *author of the historical fiction series,* A Petal In The Wind *(published by* Champlain Avenue Books*), lives on Whidbey Island with her rocket scientist husband Allan.*

THE DECISION

I know whose woods these are. They're mine, for now.

I leave the Kettles Trail to amble down the Cedar Hollow path that leads to the beach. Walking at a slowed pace, footstep after deliberate footstep, I take in the scent of pine needles mixed with decaying alder leaves and rhododendron blossoms. Thickets of salal mute the distant rumble of Friday night traffic while to the west, ablaze in a cloudless sky, the sun plays peek-a-boo through the hemlocks. Today is the summer solstice; the sun won't set until after nine and total darkness will take almost an hour to fall. I check my watch. Nearly eight-thirty. I still have time to negotiate through my woods. Tomorrow the days begin to grow shorter. No one notices, at first, but soon the dwindling hours will be evident, the long days gone.

My lungs object as I climb a steep rise, but I will continue. I like a challenge, one of the reasons I've hiked mountain trails for years, though I'm also a realist. Some paths are best left unconquered if the destination doesn't warrant the journey. That's what I must decide.

A twinge in my side jerks me and I stumble into the bushes. Snowberries dangling on wiry branches shake like fists in protest, but neither the berries nor I drop. I pat the cellphone zipped inside my hoodie pocket, my one concession to modern technology when walking alone in my woods. In case I fall. I will not answer it otherwise. This time is for me.

Ahead a fallen alder makes a natural bench and I take advantage of it. I will not be returning to the north trailhead where my husband Peter dropped me off to begin this trek. My car is parked near the beach so I have to continue downward.

I insisted on doing this and Peter reluctantly agreed. I needed some time to myself, time to relax. Time to think. Time.

Why does the world speed up as you get older? It seems like days ago when my twin daughters began kindergarten. Cuddling my infant son, I watched as my girls boarded the school bus for the first time and wondered who felt more nervous, more excited – them or me. Could twenty-five years have passed since then?

Time moves too fast now. Options are limited. That's why I'm here. When I walk in my woods, time slows down. Barriers drop.

The sky has dimmed, so I get up and continue

toward the end of the trail. I reach the water's edge, and on impulse take off my shoes and socks as I breathe in the sea air. It carries the tang of decaying seaweed, a smell I've always detested, but today it evokes a familiar coziness that brings me close to tears. I burrow my feet in the rocky sand, and as they sink in, pebbles fall into the depressions. It hurts, but in a good way. I can hear the twitter of eagles soaring above the bluff. The Parents have raised their young. The eaglets' nests sit empty now. Soon they will leave their island home for the Skagit River to fish for salmon. That is how nature intended life to be. You raise your young until they're ready to stand on their own. Then they're free to go. So are you.

I close my eyes and memorize every step, every huckleberry and hemlock, every snowberry and sword fern, every droplet of water sparkling on leaves, every mushroom and toadstool that pops up after the rain. The warm scent of cedar. The doe and her fawns darting through the Douglas firs. The ethereal effect of mist on a foggy day. The crunch of leaves beneath my feet in autumn. The hush when snow blankets the woods, the frost making clouds out of my every breath.

When I open my eyes again, these woods are no longer mine. There is no going back.

I know.

I walk barefoot to the parking lot and get into my car, turn on the headlights, and drive south toward Coupeville. A steady stream of traffic passes me in the northbound lane. Summertime weekenders from the eight-thirty ferry hoping for a taste of island life. More will arrive later, and each day thereafter all summer. Some will find their way into the woods, traverse the many paths I've traveled. They won't know me, but I will bequeath the wilderness to them.

I turn off Main Street and weave my way through the back streets until I reach my home, park in the driveway, and enter the house.

They're all waiting for me in the living room. Peter pretends to read the copy of *Time* he's holding, wishing he could fix everything and agonizing because this time, he can't. My son Matt, who has my dad's aqua eyes and my mom's straightforward nature, sits opposite Peter, staring at me, fighting his impatience. My daughter Chloe tugs at a lock of hair twirled around her finger and I flash back to the first time she did that, after getting a C in arithmetic in fifth grade. Claire sits next to her, sullen. She knows. We've always had a special connection. Her husband Joe stands at her side, as he's done since they met in high school. Claire's pregnant with my first grandchild, a girl due in early August. I'm looking forward to meeting her, maybe holding her if I still can.

Matt finally breaks the silence. "So what are you going to do, Mom? Will you try again?"

I love my family more than life itself. They won't believe me if I tell them that, so I won't. They'll know. Soon enough, they'll know.

"I've made my decision. The answer is no."

THE BACK-UP PLAN

I yawned again. We could terminate anything but boredom.

Jack fetched his penknife, a beauty with a jigged bone handle. "Guess what I saw in Hollywood today. A Rolls Royce. Never saw one up close before." He flipped the knife open and closed, open and closed, until Ed glared at him.

Jack returned the knife to his chinos. "Imagine driving around in one of them."

Ed added another stick of gum to the wad he'd been chewing, a stand-in for the Marlboros he couldn't smoke in here. "That's an old man's car. Give me a Cadillac any day."

"Cadillac wouldn't impress the ladies like a Rolls would."

Ed waggled a gloved finger. "They know nothing about cars." He turned to me. "Rob, you think the ladies would go for a guy in a Rolls over a Caddy?"

"Don't know," I said. "Me, if I bought my dream car, it'd be a '55 Porsche 550 Spyder, silver, like James Dean's."

Last year I saw one zipping around Whidbey Island, where I'm from, and it was love at first sight.

Ed nodded. "Damn fine-looking car. And coffin."

"Yeeah. Didn't he die in it?" added Jack.

I stifled a yawn. "Don't blame the car." *Yeeah.* I never could place Jack's accent.

He stood up and stretched. "Now, if you're talking sports cars, nothing beats a red Stingray in my book. No way in hell I'd buy a foreign make."

"Idiot. A Rolls is a foreign car," Ed snorted, but Jack shrugged it off.

Ed flicked his lighter on and off once, our wordless signal to begin. He picked up his two-foot length of iron pipe from the floor, and I grabbed mine. Jack shut off the light in the storeroom before opening the door. We'd been through this often enough to find our way in the dark, but within minutes our eyes adjusted, aided by street lights bleeding through the sheets of black paper covering both windows. Ed and I flanked one window like drapes while Jack peered through the other with binoculars to observe northbound traffic on La Cienega Boulevard.

Jack chuckled. "There's a Porsche about four blocks away, like the one we talked about."

"Only in Beverly Hills," Ed proclaimed. "We'll use it."

Jack narrated its progress. When the car was two hundred yards away, he said, "Aisle two, active."

Ed and I nudged the paper aside. I scanned the vehicles in the right lane until I spotted the Porsche. I aimed my pipe at it a second before Ed did the same.

"One-fifty," Jack announced. The Porsche was a hundred fifty yards away.

I took measured breaths as I focused on the car while Jack called out its approach.

"One-twenty…one-ten…."

I held the pipe steady.

"...one hundred."

Simultaneously, Ed and I pulled our imaginary triggers. We set our stopwatches, then fled the office and hurried down the skeletal staircase to the parking level, where King, Ed's tan-and-black mutt, sat patiently in a cardboard box. Ed and I stripped off our gloves and jackets. We tossed them with our pipes into a canvas bag from which Jack got out our camouflage – a tan trench coat and weathered fedora for Ed, a Bell's Valet Parking blazer for me, and a brown corduroy jacket for himself.

Ed put the leash on King as Jack unlocked the service exit, and we hurried out. Ed cut through the back alley to a residential street, masquerading as an average neighbor walking his dog. Jack carried the canvas bag to a sewer in the alley where our stuff would be dumped. I headed to the nearby parking lot and when I reached the protected niche with its bare key rack, I clicked my stopwatch and hurried back.

Jack and I met up at the bottom of the stairs that led to the service exit. Three minutes later, Ed returned, stinking of cigarettes.

Jack unlocked the door and held it open. "What took so long?"

Ed unbuckled the leash, and the dog ran back to his carton. "He had to go. So what was your time?" he asked me.

I checked my stopwatch. "Four minutes, seventeen seconds."

"Not bad. Jack?"

"Two seconds less," he bragged as he locked the

exit.

We changed clothes and returned to the top floor of an unfinished three-story building, which overlooked the main boulevard to and from the airport. Our hideout. No phones, no TV. No furniture, just some crates that would be abandoned when the job was done. Nothing to bug, tap, or trace.

"Become invisible, blend in with your surroundings."

That's what The Boss hammered into us over and over.

I look ordinary enough to work as an 'extra' in movies, and although I'm twenty-six, I could pass for a teenager. Jack, thirtyish, tall, and muscular, with a melon head and small feet, was built to carry loads. Empty-handed, he shuffled about as steady as a toddler, but during our practice drills, he moved with the agility of a dancer. Ed, craggy face and receding hairline, looked older than forty and, with his hair bleached white, you'd swear he was an old man.

The guys knew me as Rob, no closer to my real name than Ed's or Jack's. The Boss's rules. No margin for error. It's why we performed dry runs every day. Why there were two marksmen. The Boss was meticulous. Who could blame him, with an infamous plan like this.

Ed flicked his lighter on and off.

I took my position at the window, stand-in weapon in hand. The pipe weighed about the same as a high-powered rifle, which made me wonder what the real deal would be.

"What kind of 'pipes' will we be using?"

"We'll find out Saturday." Ed pointed up, which meant we'd be heading somewhere north to practice with the actual weapons. Good. I was itching to handle a real firearm again.

Back in Washington, I'd been driving The Boss's nephew Al around. We paid a visit to an auto-repair shop in South Seattle to see a loser who owed him five grand. As we got out of the car, Al handed me a .357 Magnum with a four-inch barrel.

"You expect me to need it?" I asked, hiding the pistol in my jacket.

He rolled his cigar in his mouth. "I'll handle this. You're gonna be my back-up plan."

The payout hadn't gone well. The rat knocked Al's gun away and it dropped into the pit before he split. I pulled my .357, but by the time I reached the entrance, the rat had crossed the parking bay. I took a second to aim as he scaled the chain link fence, then I fired. The rat dropped like a stone.

"He musta been eighty feet away. Lucky shot." Al laughed.

The gun had been untraceable, and I was clean, so Al let me practice with different weapons. Within a few months of training I'd become a respected marksman, perfect for the team. Once the job was done, we would remain anonymous, three more wealthy playboys lazing on some foreign beach. That's why as much effort was put into eliminating any trace of our presence in Los Angeles as in planning the job. For insurance – the back-up plan.

Jack spotted a limousine and chose it for our practice run. He called out the distances as Ed and I stood ready.

Practice ended on a positive note: Jack cut eight seconds off his best time. He began flipping his knife open and closed until a scowl from Ed made him stop.

At ten after seven, we went downstairs.

"I'm gonna take King for a walk." Ed waved good-bye, ending our workday.

Jack and I tucked behind the parking lot. When we were sure no one was around, we got into his Chevy. He dropped me at a busy intersection a mile away and drove off, leaving me to walk to Wilshire Boulevard, a major east-west route through Los Angeles. I wished I could take the car, but then again I could be freezing my ass off in Coupeville. Here, Thanksgiving's a week away and it's sixty degrees. Can't beat that.

I navigated through side streets to the bus stop, rode a while, ate dinner at a coffee shop several blocks away, and caught the next eastbound on Wilshire. I got off before downtown and wandered the streets until I reached my flop.

Around four, a chilly wind woke me. I shut the window before returning to bed. As I lay alone in the dark at this ungodly hour, my thoughts drifted into dangerous territory.

In two weeks, when my sister would be putting my nephews to bed and wondering where her bum of a husband was, when my old pals would be stumbling out of Toby's Tavern and staggering to houses strung with Christmas lights, I'd be standing by a window, waiting for a motorcade to move within a hundred-yard range.

Everyone back in Coupeville would go to bed, only to wake up the next morning to learn that the world had changed. That the man they complained about since he took office, but secretly admired, never got to his campaign fundraiser. They'd shake their heads in disbelief and pity his widow and those kids left without a father. Newspapers around the world would report the shocking story. Heads of state would attend his funeral. And none of them would ever know it was me who pulled the trigger.

I dismissed the thought immediately. Far too dangerous to form the words, even in my head. Better to stay detached. But my heart pounded so loudly I couldn't get back to sleep.

Ed had us do a run-through first thing the next morning. When we returned to the office, Jack dragged the crates out from the dark storeroom.

I sat beneath a window. "Geez, it's quiet." Traffic sounded unusually light for a Friday.

"Enjoy it while you can. It sure won't be at practice tomorrow." Ed pantomimed firing a rifle, accompanied by a gurgling sound. He checked his watch. "It's not even eleven, but my stomach's growling. Whose turn is it?"

I raised my hand. "What do you want, burgers, sandwiches?"

Jack cleaned his binocular lenses with his shirttail. "I'm kinda in the mood for Chinese."

Ed gave Jack the thumbs up. "You know a place?"

He nodded. "Less than a mile from here. He

wouldn't have to take a bus."

I memorized their orders, put on my Dodgers cap, and left through the alley. There I caught sight of it...a '55 silver Spyder with Washington plates rounding the corner. Damn, that car was fine. Part of me wanted to forget the job and follow it home, but that would be a fatal mistake.

The park across the street looked empty, so I unzipped my jacket and crossed over. The sun warmed my face as it peeked through leaves. Imagine, green leaves on the trees this late in the year. Nice, but I remained wary.

...become invisible....

This job heightened my senses, especially outdoors. When I saw how many folks wore sunglasses here, I started wearing them, too. They allowed me to study my surroundings without it looking obvious, though that was easy now. Not a soul in the park.

Even the boulevards looked deserted. No one walking, but even odder, hardly any vehicles on the road. I spotted one car pulled over to the curb, the woman inside bent over the steering wheel, weeping. An eerie silence filled the neighborhood. It creeped me out.

I cut over to a side street. It was quiet, too; no nannies walking babies or gardeners trimming hedges. The front door of a Spanish-style house flew open, and a woman ran out in tears. She crossed the street to a Craftsman bungalow and banged on the door until another crying woman let her in.

"I can't believe it," she sobbed before the door

closed.

Taking advantage of the deserted street, I snuck onto the front porch and peered inside. Several women were gathered around a television set, weeping. I couldn't see the screen so I tried to hear what had them so upset. Maybe some movie star pulled a James Dean.

I recognized the voice of Walter Cronkite.

"...from Dallas, Texas, a flash, apparently official... President Kennedy died...."

The women's gasping and tears drowned out the next few words. "Put on NBC," one urged. They quieted down as the announcer spoke haltingly.

"...after being shot...by an unknown assailant...."

My mouth hung open like a useless flap of skin. I couldn't see, or hear, or breathe until the pounding in my chest snapped me out of my daze. It all made sense now: the unnatural quiet, the woman crying in her car, the absence of people on the street and traffic on the roads.

Every person was sitting by a television or radio, learning that the world had changed.

The President had been assassinated today, two weeks before we were supposed to do the job. But who would want to kill him besides...

I ran to the curb and threw up. All the planning, the training, the elaborate ruses. All that secrecy, but we were never meant to be the main act.

We were the back-up plan.

Jack and Ed wouldn't know what happened, that Kennedy's death made us expendable...

No, worse. Targets.

We'd practiced our escape over and over, and now it would be put to the ultimate test.

I sprinted back to the office. People on the street seemed to take my behavior in stride; their faces displayed boundless compassion and immeasurable sorrow. I looked up at the covered window as I neared the building. The paper moved slightly…

Two popping noises, accompanied by flashbulbs of light, came from inside the room. Panic gripped me as I ran back to Wilshire. The eastbound bus pulled into the stop and I jumped aboard, dropped a dime in the coin box, and took a seat in the back row away from the window.

The bus lurched forward and stopped immediately as the light turned red. I counted the seconds as we waited, trying to control my breathing. At last, the red neon "Don't Walk" signal flashed on La Cienega, and I sighed aloud.

As the bus began to pull out, a gloved fist banged on the front door. Tension jolted through me like heat lightning as we stopped. I shifted over one seat. When the driver opened the door, I thrust my hand into my pocket for my switchblade knife. An elderly lady boarded. I relaxed as she sat down in the first seat as the bus moved out.

The middle-aged woman seated next to me held rosary beads as she whispered prayers. I looked past her to the window, but all I saw was my future slipping away like the storefronts on the boulevard. Where could I go? Not my flop. Or Coupeville, either, even if I wanted to; all I had in my pocket was six bucks and some change.

My edginess ramped up when I caught a sour-faced man in a gray suit staring at me. I looked away for a moment and turned back to find his eyes still fixed on my face. Beads of sweat prickled along my neck as I pulled down the brim of my cap.

Someone pulled the bell for the next stop. As the bus sailed forward, its path unobstructed by the usual midday traffic, I tried to focus on a plan rather than why the gray-suited man still held me in his gaze.

The bus driver slammed on the brakes to avoid colliding with a truck that turned in front of him, heaving the passengers forward in the process. My fists clenched as an eternity passed before the truck moved, and the bus glided through the intersection. One block away it pulled into a stop. I waited for the other passengers to exit, and at the last moment, hurried to the rear door and ran out, leaving my disturbing gawker behind.

The sun slipped behind clouds, settling a gloom on the street that matched my mood. Now what? The light turned green, so I crossed and turned west on Wilshire, hoping I'd be safer walking on a busy street. Safer from who, or how many *who*'s, I couldn't say. I studied every face I passed. They no longer looked just pained, but sullen. It made me wonder what had happened to Ed and Jack. Were they summarily executed, or interrogated first? They knew where I was going. Did they snitch me out? Maybe they weren't shot at all…maybe they made a deal to let me take the fall…maybe….

A car horn blared, and I flinched. Where was I? I'd wandered aimlessly, allowing my fears to cloud my thinking, and now I was nearly back to where I began. I had to stop thinking crazy and work out an escape…my own back-up plan.

…blend in….

Where would there be lots of folks like me? A college, like U.S.C. The campus is near downtown. Lots of people there. Perfect. I'll walk east, maybe hitch a ride along the way.

I waited to cross as a bus lumbered through the intersection. As it passed, I noticed a man on the other side of the street who wasn't there before, wearing slim dungarees and a charcoal gray pullover. He was leaning against a mailbox on the corner, his face mostly hidden behind a newspaper. Was he watching me? I lowered my head, turned around, and headed west. Paranoia crept into my gut, but I kept a steady pace until I crossed La Cienega before I dared to look over my shoulder. The man in the dungarees and pullover was following me.

Heart pounding against my ribs, I turned left and fled into familiar territory. Knowing every inch of back street and alleyway gave me a slight advantage. I veered right at the next block, trying to widen the gap between us. Every glance back found the man getting closer and closer. I searched for a place to hide, surprise him with my switchblade, until I saw him brandish a revolver that resembled a .357 Magnum. I ran even faster.

I had to do something quickly. A knife would be no match for his gun, but it would scare most drivers enough to give up their car. My best chance was the shops off Wilshire.

I cut through a back yard and dashed past a new convertible waiting in the carport, but damn, no keys. Weaving in between the houses, twisting around parked cars, I jumped fences and serpentined through driveways and alleys, all in a desperate attempt to put more distance between that gun and me. My panting came faster and harder.

The sound of a car engine idling grabbed my attention. I bolted through an alleyway toward it like a lifeline. A flash of silver metal caught my eye first. There it was…that '55 Spyder, just waiting for me less than a hundred yards away. I heard a groan behind me and looked back. Mr. Pullover had stumbled and hit the ground hard.

Somebody was watching out for me today.

I scrambled to the car, ready to jump in and race that baby away, leaving Pullover in the dust. Within minutes I'd be flying down Sunset Boulevard like a 707. Head for the beach where the kids hang out, become invisible, blend in. Yeah, this car will be my ticket. Almost there.

Inches from the door I heard the bang, then felt a sharp pain slice through my middle. I fell across the car, blood pouring out of my chest and down the door of the Porsche.

Lucky shot.

Bill Wilson

---

*With roots in the Southeast, **BILL WILSON** came to Whidbey Island in 1990 after a military career. He has degrees in English and journalism as well as an MBA. On Whidbey Bill became an award-winning journalist, a college English instructor, and marketing writer for a scientific equipment company. With wife Myrna, he spends winters in Canada skiing Big White Mountain near Kelowna, B.C., where they also volunteer for the Royal Canadian Mounted Police and for the ski resort as Snow Hosts. Bill published* Stowaway, *a literary sci-fi novella, along with stories and poems in previous WWG anthologies. He also wrote numerous news and feature stories for several Whidbey Island newspapers. Now retired from all but writing and the honey-do list, he remains a slave to the fickle muses and mountain snow fall.*

OFFICER DOWN

"Can't take this anymore," Marv remembered Sally saying, mist coating her hazel eyes, "not knowing which ring of the doorbell's gonna be the chaplain here to tell me you died a hero, just like Dave. Well, guess what? I don't need a triangle-folded flag. I need a live husband to fix leaky faucets and snuggle at the end of the day, and our kids need a father to throw a ball and bait their hooks. They sure won't get that from a black-framed photo and a brass plaque."

Every married police officer faces this kind of cloudburst at some point. Sally knew what she signed on for when she married a future cop, but seeing her friend Mary become an instant widow pushed her over the edge.

He held her and told her he understood, but being a cop was in Marv Garrett's blood. He couldn't walk away from his calling, so the opening in the Island County Sheriff's Department seemed an ideal compromise. Whidbey Island isn't crime-free, but compared to Seattle... Well, let's just say his chances of eventually retiring with a pulse looked far, far better. More important, Sally had agreed to give it a try.

Now nearing the end of his first Whidbey shift on a balmy Sunday, Deputy Garrett watches the setting sun glance off his green patrol car's windshield and scatter into the clear fall air. His shift had been quiet so far, marred only by a fix-it ticket issued to a polite sailor with a burned-out brake light. A fifteen-year veteran of the Seattle Police Department, Marv had never before experienced a duty shift like this. Though many suns setting across Elliot Bay before dipping below the Olympic Mountains rivaled the one he now took in, he rarely noticed them – rarely noticed because he always seemed to be responding to another bar fight or another suspected DWI or another gang shooting. He felt fortunate to have survived those fifteen years with only a bite scar on his wrist, courtesy of a drunken woman who objected to him arresting her abusive husband. He never discharged his weapon beyond the firing range, and he was never implicated in any of the excessive-force allegations plaguing the SPD.

Seattle now behind him, Marv sits parked beside State Route 20 not far from Deception Pass, the narrow waterway isolating his new island home from the frantic pace of the Interstate 5 corridor. While completing his shift report, he pauses to watch a gliding gull silhouetted by the last rays piercing low-lying clouds where the Strait of Juan de Fuca meets the sky. The sudden squeal of tires interrupts Marv's reverie. His radar detector beeps and flashes 75.

"What the...," he says aloud to himself as he watches a yellow BMW speed by in the northbound lane, weaving from centerline to fog line. "Oh well," he mutters to himself. "Looks like sleepy Whidbey Island just woke up." He checks oncoming traffic, activates lights and sirens, then spews dirt and gravel while executing a quick U-turn.

"Island dispatch, this is One Island forty-three northbound 20 passing Troxell Road in pursuit of yellow BMW. Speed 75, possible DUI. Couldn't get the plate."

"Roger, forty-three. Alerting WSP," replies a female voice over his radio. "Note pursuit guidelines.".

"Ten-four." Guess she assumes I'm a rookie, Marv thinks, recalling numerous aborted chases in Seattle. But the few cars on the road have all pulled off at the sight and sound of his patrol car. He's sure he's not endangering any innocents as he closes on the Beamer, his speedometer needle touching 85. "They always seem to drive bright-colored cars. Too easy."

Or maybe not so easy. The fleeing vehicle shows no signs of stopping, despite Marv's flashing lights and blaring siren. Brake lights flicker as the driver makes a hard right turn, with the deputy's vehicle following about fifty yards behind.

"Maintaining pursuit. Suspect vehicle now east-bound Ducken Road."

"Ten-four," the dispatcher's tin voice replies over the speaker. "WSP backup ten minutes out."

Speed still climbs but time slows, and Marv feels himself floating above the asphalt. In frame-by-frame succession, he merges as one with horsetail weeds and Canada thistles bending with the wind. Real time and burning rubber jerk him back to the driver's seat as the suspect's car weaves wildly from shoulder to shoulder and spins 360 degrees before coming to a stop with two wheels in a shallow ditch beside a clump of blackberries. Marv brakes hard and pulls across onto the westbound shoulder behind the yellow car, still facing east but clear of ditch and blackberries.

"Sir, step out of the vehicle with hands where I can see them," Marv says over his loudspeaker. He then reports the plate number over the radio.

"Stand by," the radio voice replies.

"Ouch!" screams the driver as he stumbles out of his car into a tangle of blackberry thorns, upsetting a swarm of bees feasting on the rotting fruit. Finally on his feet with hands above his head, the squatty-looking man stands about five feet six inches with sandy blond hair and a ruddy complexion, possibly rendered redder by alcohol. Were it not for the barrier of his squashed nose bridge, his bloodshot brown eyes might have merged and created a human Cyclops. His dimpled chin protrudes below an afterthought mouth. Definitely not Hollywood leading-man material. So he apparently has tried to offset his lack of natural assets with an expensive-looking suit, royal blue with pinstripes, now shredded by the villainous blackberry vines. *Are pinstripes still in fashion?* Marv wonders.

"Vehicle registered to a Roger Rodgers. Two priors for reckless driving."

Really, Marv thinks, *Roger Rodgers. What parent would do that? No wonder he turned to drink.*

"Careful. He has a concealed-weapon permit," the dispatcher adds.

"Ten-four," Marv answers. Then, breathalyzer in hand, he exits the cruiser and approaches Roger Rodgers, by now leaning against his trunk licking several thorn punctures on his left hand.

"What seems to be the problem, osifer?" Rodgers slurs.

"Please blow into this tube, sir."

"I will not, will not. I kn...know my r...rights."

"Very well, sir. Then I need you to walk toward me in a straight line, touching toe to heel with each step."

The man lurches toward Marv, then steadies himself and stops. "I'm n...not doing that either," he says, attempting to suppress a burp.

Marv hears the crunch of tires on gravel behind him and assumes it must be his state patrol backup. Without turning around, he again addresses the suspect. "Very well. In that case I'm arresting you on suspicion of driving under the influence of alcohol. You have the right to…"

Before Marv can finish his sentence or reach for his handcuffs, an unseen assailant jumps him from behind, knocking him to the ground.

"What the hell!" Marv sputters.

"Are you n…nuts?" he hears the first suspect say. "You can't jump on a cop."

"Beat it while you got the chance," a second voice replies.

Face to the ground, Marv struggles to free himself. He manages to flip over and come face to face with a huge man with acne scars, beer breath and a dull gaze out of sync with the fury of his fists. As the assailant repeatedly pounds on Marv's upper torso, he hears a faint but unmistakable clicking sound over the buzzing of bees around fermenting blackberries. *Round being chambered*, he thinks. *Careful. He has a concealed weapon permit… I don't need a folded flag… What cruel irony. Survive fifteen years on Seattle mean streets to be shot by a drunk beside a Whidbey Island farm field…* A circling bee distracts the assailant and interrupts the attack. While the man swats at the insect, Marv works his right hand from beneath his attacker's knee and manages to free his own sidearm and poke it into the gut of the huge man on top of him. Thus muffled, his shot sounds barely audible.

But the man's screams – screams sounding much like a braying donkey – must be heard for miles.

"You shot me, you son-of-a-bitch!" he shouts, then rolls off Marv onto his back. "I can't believe you shot me." The man grabs his bleeding abdomen while writhing and moaning.

"Shots fired! Shots fired! Officer down!" proclaims another voice from behind Marv and his assailant. "You OK, Deputy?"

Marv brings himself to one knee, then stands and brushes dirt and gravel from his uniform before facing a blue-uniformed Washington State Trooper. The trooper looks like he stepped right off a recruiting poster: white-wall haircut topped by Smokey Bear's missing hat, starched uniform, mirror-shined shoes, not to mention a weightlifter physique. His nametag reads "Burrell."

"You're bleeding," Trooper Burrell says in an almost disinterested voice, like he encounters this scene all the time.

"Not my blood. His," Marv responds, wiping more grit from his face.

"What? How? Why?" Burrell now sounds more interested, curious at least.

"Long story. First, cuff this one and call an ambulance. I'll get a compress for that wound. Pretty sure he'll live, but betting he'll think of me every time he shits for the rest of his life."

The injured assailant still lies moaning on the roadside while Marv bandages the oozing wound.

"Cancel officer down," the trooper says into his portable mike, "but dispatch ambulance for suspect.

Bill Wilson | 125

Lower abdomen bullet wound."

"I'm Marv Garrett, first day – believe that?" Marv reaches to shake the trooper's hand. "You see the other guy?"

"Jeff Burrell... What other guy?"

"The one driving that yellow Beamer. Thought he was about to shoot me after this one jumped me from behind. Coulda' swore I heard a round being chambered..."

"Not here when I pulled up," says Burrell. "Must have booked on foot."

"Least he's not drivin' anymore. Acted really drunk."

"Any idea what possessed this one to stop and jump you?"

"Coming to the aid of his drinking buddy, I guess. Never said a word to me until he screamed about being shot. You hear my weapon discharge?"

"Think so, just after I got out of the car. Pretty faint though. Didn't even spook the livestock." They both look toward several curious cows lined along the barbed-wire fence just beyond the blackberries.

"Hmm...." Marv scratches his chin. "Mind opening your vehicle door?"

"Uh, OK." The trooper shrugs then walks to his car where he opens the driver's door.

"Has to be what I heard; obviously not a round being chambered. You should lube that hinge."

APRIL 15TH

Ides of April so soon?
How can lifts lie still
and the bullwheels stop turning
while snowflakes keep falling and falling,
refusing to fade away into all those
snows of yesteryear?

Now white coats the windshield,
turning it to pale stained glass.
All the way down Big White Mountain
into the arms of waiting spring, too soon, too soon,
and the mountain mocks us winter people
not ready to let go, nor leave the snow ghosts
to haunt the Enchanted Forest alone,
not ready to endure three seasons waiting to slide
        over Kalina's Rainbow,
to plow through Powder Glades and edge down
        Paradise,
to ride the Roller Coaster and split the bumps on
        Upper Speculation
all on the way to Perfection where we're all
        Born to Run.

Yet the mountain expels us
and mocks with all that wasted snow
while seeming to say *Go home to your island,*
your season has past.

Leave me to rest and to nurture the bears and cougars,
for it is their time, the Ides of April.

Bill Wilson | 127

Barb Bland

BARB BLAND and her husband settled on Whidbey Island from Anchorage, Alaska, in 1980. She was a member of Whidbey Writers Group when it started as a spinoff from a writing class at the local senior center. After leaving WWG for several years to do artwork, she returned to get the group's guidance for writing Running Free, in which the author deals with the perils of successfully making a happy house pet of a semiferal and unsocialized young dog. "Over the Cliff" is an excerpt from this memoir. She writes short stories and poems based upon her real-life experiences. Two of her poems won prizes in the "Spirit of Writing" contest, and were published in the 2012 and 2013 editions of its magazine.

OVER THE CLIFF

A few days after I brought Piki home from the shelter, we returned from our daily late afternoon walk. I assumed that Pikachu would come from the garage into the house along with Blue. Little did I know that I would find him over the side of a 300-foot-high cliff.

I had unhooked the leash from Piki's collar, opened the car door, let the dogs out, and turned toward the door that led from the garage into the dining room. I opened it, and Blue dashed in.

There was a lull.

No Pikachu.

With a groan I realized that I had not closed the overhead garage door to confine them before I let the dogs out of the car.

Was Piki in the garden? I went back outside to look.

I didn't see him anywhere. My heart began to drum.

I called, "Pikachu!" And repeated it again, to the wind, to the birds, to the trees.

It was late afternoon, just past rush hour from the Navy base on the road behind our house, but there was still quite a bit of traffic. I knew Piki was afraid of cars, but I didn't know if he actually knew how to keep from getting hit.

I ran around the house to look for him in our backyard.

No Piki.

I looked up and down the road. He could move fast, but I wasn't that far behind him. If I couldn't see him on the road, then he was probably in a neighbor's yard.

From where I was standing I could see the yards across the road.

No Piki.

I crossed the road in order to get a better view of the yards on our side of the road.

Nothing.

Could he have crossed the road and kept going through the neighbor's back yard, over the cliff?

Impossible. He wouldn't be that dumb. I was measuring his actions by my own standards of familiarity.

But I had a gut feeling that I would find him there. Hopefully not as I had once found the body of an overexuberant Irish Setter, dashed at the bottom.

I hate heights. Dreading, I approached the edge of the sheer sandstone cliff which looks out over the beach some three hundred feet below and commands a view of the Strait of Juan de Fuca and Vancouver Island some forty miles away.

Careful not to get too close, I stopped near the edge of the vacant lot across from our house and peeked over.

There below was my new black dog, racing back and forth to the north and south ends of a six-foot-wide, fifty-foot-long grassy ledge. Its boundaries were marked by eroding striations of orange and buff sandstone in every direction, mostly in sheer drops.

My heart plummeted. In the twenty years we had lived here I had several times seen Navy Search and Rescue helicopters pluck unwary people off that cliff – drug-users hiding out, lovers looking for privacy, kids seeking adventure and tempting fate. I had even seen dogs trapped on ledges rescued by volunteer firemen roping up and going over the side after them.

Volunteer firemen! I rushed back home to phone them.

"My dog has gone over the West Beach cliff and is trapped on a ledge about thirty feet below the top. Just five houses south of Fort Nugent on West Beach Road."

Then I raced back to the cliff to wait for the firemen and to keep watch on Piki. Heart pounding, I visualized the arrival of pickup trucks bearing burly young men carrying long coils of rope. They would tie one of the men into a cradle of rope and belay him over the side as he clambered down, holding another rope for the dog....

Are you kidding? Piki would sooner jump off his ledge and try to get away than allow himself to be approached by any strange man. In what felt like an eternity, I knew this wasn't going to work.

Maybe, maybe, they would rope me up and let me go over?

Naw, not likely for macho men, I answered my own question. *Besides, they'd never believe that I, a little old lady, had had some limited experience doing this being-belayed-over before, although it had been a long time ago when I lived in Alaska.*

I ran back home, picked up the telephone, dialed 911, and cancelled the previous emergency call. Fortunately, personnel had not yet been dispatched, so they could be stopped before they left home.

Grabbing a leash, I sprinted to the cliff. Piki had stopped his frantic running and was standing still, panting heavily, the rolling whites of his eyes showing desperation. He seemed to have finally reached his own conclusion that he was in dire trouble.

"Piki," I called to him, and he looked up at me. I tried to speak softly and calmly and get him to focus on me so that he would overcome his panic. Meanwhile, I walked back and forth across the top of the cliff, searching for a place where the slope was less steep where I might be able to guide him to get back under his own power, or where I might be able to go down a little to show him the way and encourage him. He must have gone down in progressive jumps; if he had sailed out over the cliff in a single leap, his momentum would have taken him a lot farther down.

"It's OK. Just stay where you are. Don't panic. And, for God's sake, don't go any farther down." It didn't matter what I said, as I struggled to keep my voice sounding calm and confident, and maintain the connection between us.

I found soft, loose sand just below the top of the cliff behind the house to the north of where Pikachu was trapped. The loose sand only went about ten feet down, and once dislodged, it started to slide, but at least I could get a foothold. If I could keep my balance and lean into the cliff, I shouldn't slide too far down with the sand.

From that point, there were several other soft spots on the slope that led south toward Pikachu's ledge. Between them was hard, sheer rock where footholds seemed impossible, but they were not so far apart that Piki couldn't jump over them to the next soft landing place. If only he would pay attention to me as I guided him, he might be able to make it toward me on his own.

There were few handholds as I sat on the edge and eased over the side, teetering as the sand began to give way. Normally, I would have been terrified, but my attention was focused on my baby, and I knew now that only I could deal with him.

I wasn't sure Piki recognized the command "Come," but he made eye contact when he heard it. He must have judged me as being more within reach than before, so he bolted over the rock, through the sand, and into my arms so quickly that I almost fell and carried us both to the bottom.

But I didn't. I had him. And I held him tight.

Both of us panting from fear, excitement, and relief, I hooked the leash into his collar. We held our place together for a minute to compose ourselves for the final ten-foot climb. Then we turned to face it.

I knew it would be easier for Piki than for me. He could bound up the slope six feet in one jump, while the sand would slip out backwards from underneath my churning feet. But his leash was only six feet long, and I didn't want to drag him back. There was no way I was going to let go of that leash either, or he would be gone again at the top.

No more thinking. He was gone.

It all happened so fast: The leash snapped taut as Piki bounded up and away, and straining, pulled me to the top.

Disbelieving, I crawled a few feet away from the edge, and we sat near the top, catching our breath, pressed close together, physically and emotionally worn out.

After several minutes we stood, and Piki walked meekly beside me as we went back home.

Convergent Zone

Gray flannel clouds stretch from the metropolitan
    mainland,
  like sleeves covering invisible arms that reach
  beyond the shifting shoreline
  and streaming waters,
  seeking, probing, searching...

Feathery streaks of foam mirror the winds aloft,
    lead one's line of sight out to the vanishing point,
    stir and fold liquid and vapor, ultramarine and
        sienna,
    blend, bleed, mix,
    multiply shades of gray.

Nearer the shore, flatter waters circle in the cliff's
        lee:
    curling tide trails of copper and green, charcoal
        and violet,
    punctuated by dots and dashes of dark seaweed,
    patrolled by wintering mergansers with bobbing
        punk-rock hairdos;
    a black-beaked seagull nags at its long-suffering
        mother –
    Madonna and whining child.

The beach, purified by the west wind-driven
    scouring surf, lies
  healing now, its recent wounds scabbed over by
    the neutral sand,
  sifting, filtering, dropping from the deep-
    breathing sea
  to fill beside boulders, driftwood trunks, tangled
    kelp,
  to soothe and soften the stark wreckage of
    carcasses
        shell   weed   bone   wood   seed   stone

Footprints show that here Otter Noster waddled out
    of the brine
  to drink sweetness seeping from the cliff's
    textured rock strata,
  and the nervous-fingered raccoon washed
    breakfast in clear water;
  there, salt-savoring deer bounded up impossible
    slopes,
  to vanish like the morning fog.

Rising on an updraft, a broad-shouldered eagle
    glides past
  fir trees clinging to the cliff's upper edge, clawing
    their roots
  into fickle sandstone, postponing the concussion
  that will break and blunt their limbs as,
  senseless at the bottom, they will dam the shifting
    sands.

Atop the cliff, at eagle's-eye level, young Webelos
        are too engrossed
    in tracking candy-wrapper clues on worn park
        paths
    of The Forest Primeval to notice the eagle's
        sidelong glance
    or to see an unseen finger poke a distant hole
    in the scudding gray fabric sky

    and pull threads that fast unravel a seam,
    exposing the naked blue skin of infinity.

DANGLING

wait for

look over

think about

pick out

pay for

wrap up

take along

figure out

set up

try out

play with

report to

take back

what if

Karen Rothboeck

A native Oregonian, for the last 30 years **KAREN ROTHBOECK** *has lived on Whidbey Island where she worked in a medical office and later managed a veterinary clinic. She wrote human interest stories and a monthly book review column for* The Coupeville Examiner *(later* The Whidbey Examiner*) from 1998 to 2008. Since her retirement in 2014 she has devoted her time to writing and teaching yoga.*

LOST AND FOUND

Along the Methow River the aspen glowed like beacons in the late October light. The first layer of snow settled on Mt. Washington. In a few weeks, Highway 20 would close. The Silver Star Gate would clang shut, locking the residents of Winthrop in for the winter.

The short-order cook for the Gateway Grill stood outside the restaurant smoking a cigarette, his ample middle swaddled in a grease-stained apron. He took a look over the false-front buildings toward the mountain peaks and assessed the looming weather as he dropped his cigarette and ground it out on the wooden boardwalk.

The waitress glanced out the window. "Gavin!"

she yelled, flagging down a young man who was walking past with a scruffy-looking terrier on a leash. "I have a job for you."

Gavin stopped and waited as the waitress darted to the kitchen and returned with two Styrofoam take-out boxes. "This top one needs to be delivered to the ice-cream store, and the bottom one is some scraps for your dog."

The restaurant didn't pay Gavin to deliver food to nearby shop owners, but most merchants gave him a generous tip. He looked as if he could use the money. As his lanky body disappeared down the boardwalk, the wind pasted his thin maroon T-shirt to the prominent vertebrae of his spine.

He dropped off the warm sandwich at one shop and headed next door to the antique store. Still on the porch, he opened the second container, fished out a piece of ham for himself, and left the rest of the scraps for Hobo.

Gavin entered the store, removed his backpack, and set it on the front counter. "I brought you something," he said. He pulled out a couple of newspaper-wrapped parcels, which contained two glass bottles aged by time and sunlight to a lovely lavender color.

This was how Gavin supported himself, selling found items and doing odd jobs. When the items were obviously cast-offs, the antique store proprietor would buy them. However, there had been a rash of burglaries in town, and she had said "no" to his offerings of an antique emerald ring and a delicate hand-painted oil lamp.

More than once Gavin had bragged to townsfolk that he was going to hit it big. He carried a well-worn college diploma in the outer pocket of his pack. Practically falling apart at the folded and refolded seams, it proved he had a degree in geology. He made no secret of the fact that he prospected for gold in the hills and canyons above town.

No one was sure where he slept, although someone remembered that the first time they saw him, he had a tent and sleeping bag tied to his pack. No one knew how he survived, although certainly he got handouts from local restaurants, and once or twice he was seen picking through a garbage can or Dumpster. He always said this was only so he could feed Hobo.

Gavin was like a neighborhood cat, someone everyone assumed belonged to someone else but didn't mind feeding once in a while.

He was secretive and not above suspicion. The break-ins left people nervous. In an unrelated incident, the town marshal was called to the brewery one night after a brawl that Gavin would not admit to initiating but couldn't deny being involved in, as his rapidly blackening eye testified for him.

One night at the bar Gavin overheard a story that intrigued him. An old-timer told a tale he'd probably told dozens of times before about an abandoned homestead.

The geezer, as Gavin thought of him, told the story like this:

Once when I was a kid, two of my friends and I were out on our horses, just following our noses and looking for some excitement.

My friends remembered an old house way up one of these draws. They called it the Yellow House, although you practically needed a magnifying glass to find a speck of old yellow paint. It was awfully weathered and beat up – no glass in the windows, a rotted-out porch.

We had fun poking around and wondered if the well had any water in it. We tried to pry off some old pieces of lumber that covered it. When we levered up a board, those rusty nails coming out made a godawful screech.

Suddenly we heard a bit of a commotion from the house. We had no idea what we'd see when we turned around, but a big old mountain lion must have been sleeping up in the attic. He was just as surprised as we were, and he jumped clean from that second story to the ground and then went tearing out of there.

Gavin had been absolutely reeled in by that story. The yellow house became a sort of fixation and he convinced himself that if he could find the house, it would be the beginning of a change in his luck. He hung out in the bar until closing time and followed the old man home.

The next day he came back, offering his services: Did the lawn need mowing or the leaves need raking? He worked to cultivate a friendship and to make the old guy bring up the story in a way that didn't seem as if Gavin had wrung it from him. Soon Gavin had a rough idea of what direction he'd need to head.

Armed with a USGS map, Gavin began his search. After several wrong turns, wasted hikes, and an unexpected overnight trip, he found the old place. Not only did Gavin find the house, he found an old mine nearby that yielded a bonanza.

He filed and recorded a claim. There were moments when he'd held his breath, but it looked as if the mineral rights were his. Next he would work to see if he could own the property also.

October was at an end. Fall and the closing of the gate into town were so near that Gavin needed to act soon.

Thoughts of fortune and owning the old yellow house went through Gavin's mind as he approached the property on a trail that became more familiar to him every time he hiked it. He walked to the old one-seater outhouse built of wide planks that would have let in an uncomfortable amount of snow, wind, or whatever other weather came calling. The door hung by a rusty hinge.

Gavin donned a pair of heavy leather gloves. He creaked the door open and gently pried up the plank that formed the inside seat of the outhouse. He carried the board outside, flipping it upside down. Tacked to the underside of the plank was a small leather bag. He felt safer hiding it here than keeping it in his backpack.

He took another look around. The only other breathing creature in sight was Hobo. Gavin removed his gloves and loosened the rawhide drawstring of the bag, shaking a large gold nugget into the palm of his hand.

Gavin thought so often about this nugget he'd found in the old mine that it had acquired its own personality. He named it Old Granddaddy and many times promised Old Granddaddy he'd come back for him.

He marveled at the story that started all this, the one he'd heard in the bar about an old homestead and a mountain lion: a big tawny cat in a big yellow house unknowingly guarding a golden bonanza.

Maybe the same thing that had drawn those boys up here years ago had drawn Gavin also.

He heard the pad of feet behind him and turned to see Hobo nosing around in the dirt. They'd spend a lot of time up here. He'd call his claim the Lucky Cat Mine. He could sense a magical presence around the place.

Hobo started barking, and Gavin turned, unintentionally exposing the soft flesh of his throat to a leaping mountain lion. For a split second he wondered whether he had somehow thought or imagined the cat back into being.

He fought bravely but unsuccessfully. The last sound he heard was Hobo's frustrated bark. In the shock of the attack, Gavin had dropped Old Granddaddy. The nugget rolled gently down the hill and stopped at the base of a fire-blackened pine tree, joining a spill of a million other rocks.

All winter Gavin's bones lay outside, first exposed to scavengers, then neatly tucked in under a blanket of snow. The day came when the aspen trees wore their spring-green gowns, and new growth clothed the ground. Birds switched to their mating songs, and the bones re-emerged with the wildflowers, but still no one came to the house.

Once in a while, someone from town would think of Gavin and wonder what he was doing now, assuming he must have left town before the gate closed for the winter.

Several ridges over from the old yellow house, a farm family had a new dog, a stray who showed up cold and hungry at the door just before the first snow. He lived with them many years, following them on trail rides and keeping the property free of rats. He spent a lot of time in the barn, although he took care to avoid the cats. Sometimes he crept over to lap cream from their old tin pie plate, but at the first glare from an amber eye he went quickly on his way.

THE HAPPINESS VIRUS

Melinda knew it would be a bad day at work the moment she heard someone yelling for the disposable hug-restraints.

Had the virus already penetrated their field office? She hesitated with one hand on the doorknob, weighing her options, then pushed herself all the way in. The strap of her bag slid off her shoulder, drawing the neckline of her white lab coat off her shoulder also.

She dropped her bag on her desk, straightened her coat, and looked around. Two other employees had Bob backed into a corner and were holding him there with a straight-backed chair wielded in lion-tamer fashion.

A third employee bustled into the office triumphantly waving the strappy affair dubbed "the hug-restraint."

Melinda sighed. "Someone's going to have to suit up," she said. "And is anyone feeling as if they may have already been exposed? Any hugs or kisses?" she asked with her hands on her hips, eyes fixed in a piercing glare.

There were meek shakings of heads. Melinda pointed to the other female in the office. "You. Find a suit."

While they waited, Melinda turned to Bob.

"Bob, Bob. What are we going to do with you?"

Bob was an employee notable for his lack of wit, warmth, or basic social skills. He still wore tortoise-shell glasses with huge square yellow-tinted lenses. His mustache was a similar vestige from the eighties. He'd been drinking Sanka from the same Snoopy mug for the past fifty years.

Now just days away from retirement he'd caught the bug. There was no denying it, because Bob was in the corner exhibiting all of the classic symptoms.

"I love you all so much!" Bob made an attempt to reach past the chair legs holding him at bay. "I woke up this morning knowing something was different. I felt like I was looking through rainbows, seeing a sunshiny new world.

"I put on my clothes and it's as if they're all stitched in gold. I glow, don't I? Don't I just glow? Did I tell you about breakfast? I've never eaten a fresher, more delicious egg in my life. And my coffee this morning: It's elixir, absolute fountain-of-youth stuff ... "

Bob blathered on, but Melinda's attention was diverted by the door opening and the now fully protected figure of her fellow employee cautiously emerging.

"All right, let's make this quick," Melinda said. With the other two continuing to hold Bob at bay with the chair, the one-woman hazmat crew waded in with the disposable hug-restraint.

It was no job to buckle up Bob. He was so happy to have someone to hug that he let himself be bound, occasionally interrupting the process with little kisses, love pats, or exclamations along the line of "glorious, glorious day!"

Melinda didn't interrupt until she was certain Bob was secure. "Is the PNW room ready?" she asked.

Unanimous nods assured her that it was ready. "Take him there," she said in a terse voice. "I'll wait until the decontamination team gets here. And you two need to head straight for the showers."

She glanced at the clock on the wall. Just another seven and three-quarters hours of this hellish day left. She paused, played back her thoughts, and nearly guffawed. At least with an attitude as dark as hers, she could be pretty damn sure she wasn't infected yet.

It bothered Melinda they had nothing more to offer than the PNW room, a mere treatment of symptoms rather than a cure. It had been the brainstorm of an employee in the Seattle region who had noticed that the outbreak seemed a little milder there, the victims less manic.

Now all regional field centers had a Pacific Northwest room, a controlled environment that was cold, dark, and damp. It literally and figuratively dampened the enthusiasm of those struck by the Happiness Virus.

But what could PNW be but a stopgap measure when the mortality rate on this damned bug was ninety-something percent? Never had Melinda dealt with an illness this severe, where people were purposely exposing themselves.

"They know better!" she blurted to no one except herself. Then she thought of Bob, a white-collar worker, a statistician with few hobbies other than occasional target-shooting at the local rifle range. The virus transformed him into a joyful figure with a glow like an old Renaissance oil painting of an angel lighting on earth.

She guessed she could understand a little of what onlookers were thinking when they decided they needed that disease too. But still, what was the world coming to when someone would rather die happy than continue living unhappily?

Melinda stood beside her desk and idly thumbed through the latest stack of reports in her inbox. The method of infection had been confirmed and was as insidious as anything she'd experienced in her life of medical research.

It was the virus making people happy – contagiously happy. As the exuberant victims felt an uncontrollable urge to hug, to kiss, to share their joy, the virus shed. The victim served his purpose and died, but by then the virus already had a new host.

At least throwing people into the PNW rooms kept them away from healthy remnants of the herd. After about half a day in the room, victims returned to a fairly subdued state. This allowed well-protected medical personnel to enter and draw blood for testing and avoid being seduced by a level of enthusiasm they found themselves thinking they must experience too.

In the earlier days of the outbreak, with less known about the disease and the PNW rooms not yet in use, one of Melinda's close associates had torn off his protective gear in an isolation room at the urging of a patient who had asked, "How can I give you a real hug through that glass and plastic suit?"

Melinda guessed the patient had appeared to be the world's most huggable patient, and most insistent also. A siren interrupted her melancholy remembrance of those events. Either someone had escaped from PNW or...

She ran toward the door that led into the back rooms of the center, looked up and down the hallway, and saw some sort of commotion down by the showers. She knew she should grab a suit, but the urgency of the situation seemed to override protocol. The yelling was getting louder.

Large glass double doors led into an air-lock entry of sorts, and from there a second set of doors led into changing rooms and decontamination showers. She stopped to peer through the glass. A tile wall blocked her from seeing into the showers, but she could hear singing coming from that area, an off-key rendition of "Moon River."

One of the employees she'd sent to the shower stuck his wet head out from around the tile wall and looked straight back through the glass at her. She could read his lips: "Come on in, the water's fine!"

Melinda moved her hand to the keypad that would seal off the whole shower/decontamination area from the hallway and front office, and effectively lock in the bathers.

The singer stuck his head around the tile wall a second time. He spread his arms wide, signifying a wish to wrap her in an embrace. He had a towel wrapped around his middle and grinned and re-knotted it when it began to slip down.

A second figure emerged from the ladies' dressing area. She was naked and unembarrassed by her nudity. She was holding a shampoo bottle, and pointed to it with her other hand. "Smells like strawberries," Melinda thought she said.

The two people had been emerging alternately from the dressing rooms like two figures on the platform of a cuckoo clock, but suddenly they noticed each other. They hugged like long-lost cousins, and waved again at Melinda.

Her hand was still on the pad of the locking mechanism. She told herself not to look at the shower area again; her last glance had shown her colleagues absolutely glowing with happiness. Melinda didn't believe in auras, but she could swear she saw them now – or halos, or some kind of strange New Age stuff.

Movement caught her eye. Someone had let Bob out of PNW, and nearly instantaneously he snapped out of his lab-induced depression.

The three in the decontamination unit played ring-around-the-rosie and sprawled on the floor in gentle, giggly hysterics. Melinda could see Bob was beginning to tire. The disease moved so quickly it was like watching a car brought to a shuddering halt by someone standing on the antilock brakes.

She smiled at the antics of her other two friends. She was thinking about brake lights, that brake lights meant...that red meant.... She giggled. Her hand slid away from the door lock to waggle her fingers at the window in a playful wave.

THE GREAT ZOMBIE WAR

"Grandpa, what did you do in the Great Zombie War?"

The white-haired man reached down and tousled his grandson's hair, smiled, and said in a not very gruff tone, "Seems to me I've told you that before."

"But I want to hear it again, Grandpa."

"You see Zeke over there?" Grandpa pointed a trembling finger to a character bent nearly double in his wheelchair.

Ned followed his grandfather's finger until his eyes settled on Zeke. He didn't want to say it to his grandpa, but there were days Ned was convinced Zeke was slowly turning into a zombie himself – the worn and tattered clothes, the nearly transparent skin, the slack-jawed gaze.

"Zeke and I were best friends," Grandpa said, paused, and then added, "and still are. Look at us, living here together at the war veterans' home. You might find it hard to believe, but we were once two of the top zombie fighters during the Whidbey Outbreak."

"Tell me again about the outbreak."

"Well, it was a long time ago. You're twelve now, right? We were just four years older than you. Nowadays we'd probably be considered too young to fight. Maybe even then it would have been a problem except everything happened so fast.

"Zeke and I had this harebrained idea that we'd like to spend a night at Sunnyside Cemetery. We snuck...I mean, our parents had given us permission to take our sleeping bags and a backpack full of food and gear up to the cemetery. We waited for a night there was a full moon and set off to fulfill something we'd dared each other for a long time: to be brave enough to spend the night in the old blockhouse. I wonder if it's even still there," Grandpa mused.

"It is, Grandpa. I was just up there on a school field trip. We heard about how Isaac Ebey got his head chopped off, and they built the blockhouse in case there were more attacks from warring tribes. And there's even a man named Fred Krueger buried at Sunnyside."

"I knew Fred," Grandpa said.

"Anyway, nothing went the way we planned. Zeke's kind of a scaredy-cat..."

"Am not," came a feeble voice from nearby. A nurse in cheerily flowered scrubs was pushing Zeke past them toward the dining room.

Grandpa let Zeke roll out of earshot and continued his story. "First an owl, a great-horned owl, flew right out of a tree and into our faces. We...er, Zeke was already feeling pretty shook up after that, and then the fog rolled in.

"You know how that can be: cold, clammy fingers of fog sneaking through the tree branches, covering the ground, making a person feel like a mummy wound in wet gauze. Nothing looks familiar. We were at the blockhouse by then and ready to go inside when Zeke said, 'Stop pushing me!'"

"And I said, 'I didn't push you!' And then Zeke said, with his eyes really wide, 'Well then, who?'

"At that moment I realized we were in the middle of an earthquake. With the moon out and a sudden break in the fog, we could see the prairie below us rolling like long ocean waves. The trees were swaying back and forth, and it was hard to stay on our feet. I thought it lasted probably ten minutes, and Zeke guessed fifteen. We found out later it was more like a minute, but it sure didn't seem like it at the time.

"The worst was yet to come. The earthquake opened a long downhill rift in the cemetery. It split grave markers in half and tossed headstones around like popcorn. It was almost some kind of chain reaction – the owl like an omen, the fog, the earthquake, and then..."

"Ready for lunch?" a kindly nurse asked him, her hands already on the back of his wheelchair.

"Well, sure, I'd like lunch. What do you say, Ned? I'm sure they'll rustle up something for you, too."

Ned would have eaten anything, even vegetables, at this point, he was so engrossed in the story, and he obediently followed his grandpa into the dining area.

"Tell me more, Grandpa!"

"Maybe I shouldn't. Is this going to interfere with your sleep tonight?"

"No way!"

"OK. When the ground cracked open, it allowed the undead to leave their graves and walk the earth. The very earth of Coupeville. First Zeke and I could hardly stand up due to the earthquake, and then it was like we were glued to the spot and couldn't move, even though we wanted to. Imagine seeing the zombies heaving themselves out of the ground, shaking off the dirt of the graves, and emerging with a taste for fresh blood.

"There Zeke and I were by that blockhouse, and it didn't even have a door on it anymore." Grandpa manipulated a salt-and-pepper shaker across the table to indicate his and Zeke's positions. "Back then – and we might have been the first ever to see any zombies – we didn't know what might attract or repel them.

"Zeke gave me a boost, and I scrambled onto the blockhouse roof; then I lowered my arms and helped him get up." At this point Grandpa had the salt and pepper balanced precariously on top of a stainless steel napkin dispenser. Ned had a forkful of mashed potatoes lifted halfway to his mouth, but it seemed frozen there.

"Zeke was wriggling out of his backpack and lost his grip on it. It slid off the roof, and that's when we found out it was noise that attracted zombies. They all homed in on us like hornets after a kid who threw rocks at their nest. We figured our only hope was if they couldn't climb, but something else happened to divert them.

"There was a sudden crack of thunder and a bolt

of lightning, and we could see all the lights in the town below us go out. The noise was enough to turn the zombies in that direction. Not too long after that, we heard a siren and could see flashing lights. They used that as a beacon and abandoned us for something they thought might be more interesting."

"That's just like in the movies, Grandpa!"

Grandpa paused and scratched his chin, savored the turkey and stuffing he was eating, and thought a moment. "You know, Ned, it wasn't really much like the movies. For one thing, in the movies, the zombies can only move really slowly, and they're clumsy and not too smart. But not only were they fast and able to learn from their mistakes, they could copulate."

"Copulate?"

"Er, yes, populate. Repopulate. They could have baby zombies that grew to adulthood in an incredibly short period of time. It seemed like no sooner did we kill a slew of 'em than we'd find another nest."

"But how did you get rid of them? Did you use swords and guns? Cannons? Did they eat everyone in Coupeville?" Ned asked.

"Those were sad times," Grandpa said, shaking his head. "You know what a quarantine is?"

"Yeah, like the Ebola quarantine of 2020," Ned said with a grin. "Eight weeks of no school."

"Well, all the shops on Front Street closed. People were warned to stay in their homes. There were shortages of food, although the braver and hungrier folks ventured out to gather shellfish off the beach or shoot deer. Some lost their lives that way, getting attacked unawares. Others were caught out when that first big wave of zombies hit Coupeville. Some of my best friends died that night at a football game, with the field being so close to the cemetery and the lights being out and the zombies suddenly just everywhere. A lot of us were angry. We wanted to defend the town and save lives and get rid of the zombies. We had one big advantage."

"You were here on Whidbey Island, right, Grandpa?"

"Yessir, and people here had their heads on straight. Immediately they stopped the ferries running on the South End and to Port Townsend. Up north they barricaded Deception Pass bridge and mounted shifts of armed guards. Some hotheads on the mainland wanted to blow up the bridge to protect themselves, but we proved we could control the outbreak without those kinds of extreme measures.

"You know, the Zombie War was how I lost this," Grandpa said, pointing dramatically to his left leg, an obvious prosthesis. "I was in the jaws of a zombie and Zeke pulled me loose, but then they had to cut off the leg to save me from zombie toxin."

Ned blurted out, "Grandma always said that was your Dia-Beegees."

Grandpa shook his head in a pitying fashion. "I think you were a little tender for her to tell you the whole truth. She was protecting you, Ned."

Ned opened his mouth with another question, but saw his mom walking toward them.

"Hi, Dad," Ned's mom said, wrapping her arms around her father and giving him a hug. "I got all of that stuff you asked me to do taken care of. The staff hauled out that old maple dresser. Another resident down the hall already asked if she could have it. I brought the longer phone cord so the phone will reach as far as the bed in case you want to call me late at night. And I got the old police scanner hooked up. That thing's such an antique I hardly believed it would work anymore!"

"Thanks, darling," her father replied. "I sure enjoyed having Ned here to keep me company while you did all that. We had a great talk." He put his index finger to his lips and signaled silently to Ned that the less said about the subject of the talk, the better.

"Well, Ned and I had better be taking off, Dad. Want me to roll your chair over to Zeke's table?"

"Sure," her father said. "Just park me next to him and I'll be fine. Ned, now that I've got the phone set up, don't be surprised if you get a call from me."

Ned ran over and gave Grandpa a hug. What a great character Grandpa was. Imagine him coming up with all of those crazy zombie fairy tales just to entertain his grandson. Ned looked back and gave Grandpa a final little wave as he and his mom headed toward the exit.

"Zeke," Grandpa said as he turned to his long-time friend and fellow resident. "I've got the scanner. We're not going to have to feel so isolated here anymore."

"Here, I managed to get another one of these," Zeke said in a whisper, passing Grandpa a butter knife. Both of them reached into their cardigan pockets and pulled out matching knives sharpened to a lethal point, a sign of meticulous hours of work with a whetstone. They crossed knives discreetly.

"One for all and all for one," Zeke said.

"Kids," Grandpa countered. "May they always believe the Zombie Wars are over."

Upstairs, the housekeepers used the time the residents were in the dining room to do some light cleaning. In Grandpa's room, one of them swiped a feather duster over an ancient machine she hadn't noticed before. It crackled to life. *Reports of a disturbance at the cemetery. Graves found open....* She bent to tighten the sheet corners. Nothing to do with her.

Gordon M. Labuhn

GORDON M. LABUHN, *born in Detroit, Michigan, has written and produced a nationally publicized movie and twelve one-hour religious vignettes; he has published a business management book, murder mysteries, a memoir, and a story in an animal anthology. For three years he was a monthly feature article writer for a Detroit area newspaper. Gordon was winner of a national PR/PI research award, and the Whidbey Island Classic Car Show Writing Competition. His most recent publications can be viewed on Amazon and his website, labuhnbooks.com.*

DIFFERENT STROKES

Amelia's cat Muffy perched on the arm of the sofa purring as Amelia talked about Floyd, the newspaper editor. "Can you believe this may be my last day of work? Floyd plans to fire me because he doesn't like the stories I write? It's not my fault. He sends me on an assignment, I write the story. He reviews, approves, and prints it, then has the gall to tell me no one is interested in the stories I write. I'm a good writer. He doesn't give me a chance to write about important things that are happening in the world – things people care about. What does he expect? I can embellish a dull subject just so much.

"I'm not paid enough, either. I can make more money teaching in the public school, and believe me, teaching is one of the worst-paying jobs in this small burg they call a city. This is hardly a big town, let alone a city," complained Amelia.

"All I need is a little time. Is that too much to ask? I don't think so!" She prattled on and on.

Muffy purred and washed while Amelia relieved her stress by banging about preparing breakfast. Amelia talked incessantly, and Muffy purred louder exponentially to the length of Amelia's morning incantations. This was their daily breakfast ritual.

"My editor's an egomaniac, proud of his big office, cherry desk, and executive chair elevated on a platform. Gloats over his private parking space, and constantly shows off his stupid baseball signed by Mickey Mantle. His office isn't big enough for his ego. You want chicken or salmon this morning?"

Amelia continued expounding on her newspaper career frustrations and dreams.

"Sometimes I hate this job. They treat me like some kind of a spastic nut bag, but you just wait and see! One of these days I'm going to hit it big. I'll write a story that will curl your fur. It will be international news. Then we'll see how high and mighty that bobble-head is.

"Muffy, you want a little of each? And another thing: Once I'm rich, I'm going to move out of this dumpy town to New York, or maybe San Francisco. I'm going to live high on the hog. Muffy, believe me, I'm going to live in style."

Amelia continued her tirade about her rotten boss. While the sausage sizzled so did she. She poured coffee onto her plate of eggs and scalded her left hand.

"Dag-nabbit!" she screeched. She drained the coffee from her plate into the sink. One egg slid off the plate, but with a desperate grab, she saved it from disappearing down the garbage disposal. She flopped the slimy mess back onto her plate. Amelia then overfilled her coffee cup and spilled some on the counter. Seating herself, she bumped the table leg and tipped over her coffee cup, which crashed to the floor.

"I forgot a fork."

Amelia rose, ignoring the broken cup and coffee, and tipped her chair over. She stumbled, twisted, and grabbed the edge of the sink. Miraculously she remained upright. She retrieved a fork from the dirty pile of dishes in the sink, picked up the chair, and sat down only to discover that she had left her muffin in the toaster and forgotten the jam. Amelia brushed aside the broken cup with the side of her foot, and salvaged a blackened English muffin and a jar of raspberry jam with a thin layer of mold on its surface.

"Last week they had a big explosion at the Calumet copper mine: a fire, cave-in, trapped miners, the whole nine yards. It was a great opportunity for national coverage. I begged Floyd to let me do the story, but no; he assigned a snot-nosed kid of twenty-one who couldn't find his way out of a bag. Hell, he couldn't find his way into a bag. His story was awful, and Floyd didn't say a word to him about it. Then

Floyd has the audacity to say I'm not a good reporter. He doesn't give me a chance to show what I can do."

How Amelia could talk so much and still get anything done was a wonder.

"Muffy, are you ready to go outside and do your potty thing? Are you done washing? I'll probably be late getting home tonight. I have to stop at the grocery store. You better go out now before I leave for work."

Reverting to her favorite theme, Amelia steamed onward.

"You know, Floyd has become a male chauvinist pig. He doesn't think women should work, and he's trying to drive me away. Well, it's not going to work. I'm going to figure out some way to stay. You wait and see."

Amelia continued to talk while she was eating.

"I want to go visit Europe someday and see the Eiffel Tower, and the Louvre to see all the famous paintings and sculptures. A month-long cruise down the Amazon would be fun too. Flying in the supersonic jet would have been a blast. I wish they were still in service. Once Floyd recognizes my abilities, I'll be in money heaven. Just think, I'll be able to go anyplace I want."

Amelia was like a ventriloquist. She could eat and talk at the same time and not appear to be eating at all. The food on her plate seemed to evaporate.

"I've lost my car keys again."

In a frantic search, Amelia shifted newspapers from the coffee table to the floor, and scattered a stack of unopened mail. She checked clothing draped over the couch and coffee table. The search included the overflow of dirty dishes in the sink, and half-filled coffee cups found in nearly every room. She found her keys in plain sight at the end of the kitchen counter.

Floyd, her editor, classified Amelia with car and insurance salesmen, considering her a pushy, inconsiderate, self-centered, money-grubbing rogue. He claimed Amelia had been drained of compassion and kindness, and that the success dragon was slowly burning up her soul.

"I'll leave the dishes and do them later; but Muffy, you need to go out now."

Amelia pushed reluctant Muffy out the back door, and then climbed the steps two at a time in a mad dash to her bedroom.

The contrast between Amelia's outside appearance and inside reality was astounding. The inside of her home and mind were in disarray, while her outside appearance was refined and orderly. Within moments Amelia reappeared, fully groomed and looking like the establishment's prima donna businesswoman stepping off the front cover of *Business Week*.

As Amelia came down the stairs, she tripped and nearly fell. She clutched the railing, and her body pivoted into the wall with a resounding thump.

"Darn! I think I bruised myself," she blurted out.

After readjusting her blouse, she marched like a tin soldier down the last three steps.

Amelia let Muffy in and lovingly picked her up

for a brief petting. Amelia took a deep breath. "I love you, Muffy." She gently set her cat down in a cushioned bed.

"I gotta go," Amelia announced.

She stumbled down the side porch steps, safely negotiated six round steppingstones to the garage, and backed out her old dinosaur Buick Limited. There was a horizontal crease across the trunk where she had closed the garage door before the car was fully inside.

Amelia floored the gas pedal and squealed the wheels backward down the driveway. She jammed on the brakes, screeched to a stop, and again peeled rubber as she leaped forward in first gear. There was enough rubber on the driveway to make another tire.

At the newspaper office, Floyd ordered Amelia to come into his office. He fumbled nervously with a tension squeeze ball when Amelia entered.

"Amelia, I've treated you badly. I'm sorry. Now I may be joining you in the unemployment line. That damn egotistical owner, Richard the Wimp, wants to fire me. I'm embarrassed to ask, but what do you think I should do?"

Amelia was dazed but somewhat mollified. Maybe Floyd was OK after all.

She advised: "Egotistical bastards need recognition and praise. Give him your office and desk as a peace offering. Let him use your special parking space, and give him a gift of your signed Mickey Mantle baseball. You might want to give him front-page coverage as the paper's grand patriarch. That should do it."

Richard already owned the office and parking space, but he appreciated the gesture and the autographed baseball. Floyd kept his editor position, though he was now seated at a metal desk in the pressroom. In appreciation, Floyd didn't terminate Amelia, and he gave her prime story assignments.

Richard, when he learned of Amelia's praise of his esteemed ownership position, granted her the use of his big office and cherry desk any time he was not using it.

Muffy had both salmon and chicken for dinner, regularly.

My Woman Elizabeth

There is only a spark plug gap between the love and hate I have for a piece of tin that joyously gnaws away at my time and patience. My woman, at the age of ninety, stills limps along, trying to keep up with today's 45 mph speed demons. She's a little shaky on her wooden spindles, she's hump-backed, and her front boasts two magnificent kerosene falsies, pretending to light the way.

My woman is cranky and tries to break my thumb when I wake her up. She dies often, but revives and lives again, with a loud and rhythmic heartbeat. She's had so many surgeries that most of her parts belong to someone else. Her ribs of wood creak, and her glass nose turns red when she's steaming mad. Supplies for a liquid diet are hidden beneath her seat. Shouting *ooougaaa* frightens chickens and makes children laugh. Occasionally she passes gas with a shattering bang. It's embarrassing!

She has a colorful personality even though her canvas top hat and dress are black. I spend a great deal of time on my back working on her bottom. My woman is a knuckle-smashing, arm-twisting, thumb-breaking, aggravating American icon.

The little old lady gives me grief almost beyond endurance, yet I truly love to escort my Model "T" Turtle Back Roadster in the Fourth of July parade. She is both my nemesis and my Queen of Hearts. That's my Liz!

"My Woman Elizabeth" was the First Place prize-winner in the Bayview, Washington, Classic Car Show Writing Competition.

Λ Ω

TRAVELING HOME

19ᵀᴴ Century Haiku Japanese Poetry

17 syllables divided into three non-rhyming phrases, 5,7,5 written in one line.

"Snuggled warm water, little steps bruises, school zits, rings white hair dark dirt."

19th Century Haiku American Poetry

17 syllables divided into three non-rhyming phrases, 5,7,5, written in three lines.

> Snuggled warm water
> Little steps bruises school zits
> Rings white hair dark dirt

New Generation Haiku Poetry

20th Century non-rhyming phrases divided
5,7,5,7,5,1,1 two single words as punch line.

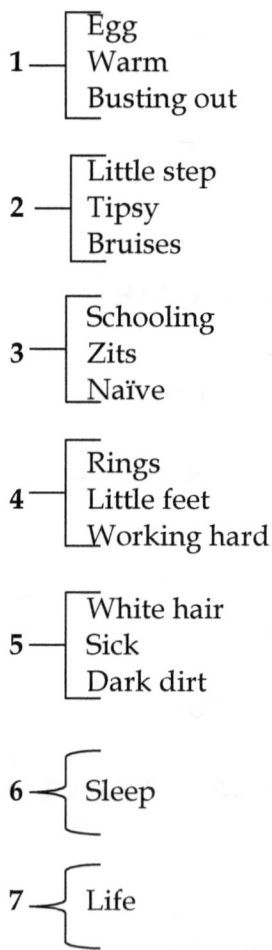

1 —
- Egg
- Warm
- Busting out

2 —
- Little step
- Tipsy
- Bruises

3 —
- Schooling
- Zits
- Naïve

4 —
- Rings
- Little feet
- Working hard

5 —
- White hair
- Sick
- Dark dirt

6 — Sleep

7 — Life

Art work and poetry are interpreted by the viewer and reader. Often the interpretation is not the same as what the artist and poet had in mind, but this is one of the beautiful aspects of these forms of communication. What brings one person to tears may cause another to smile. The more abstract a painting or the fewer the words in poetry, as in Haiku poetry, the greater the possibility of variance in the readers' and writers' interpretations.

Read the poem on the previous page and enjoy your own understanding of its content. Discover the writer's mind set by completing the word puzzle below.

1 to 7 Across: Stages corresponding to each of the 7 stanzas of the poem.

8 Down: A family member of a symbolic biblical enemy of 7.

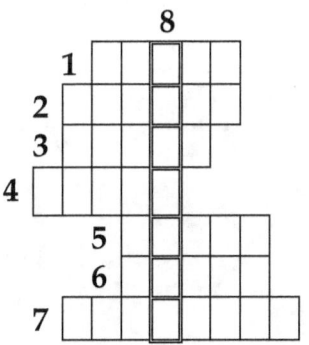

Answers to puzzle on page 207.

Nasus Nunn

"NASUS" *is the pen name that has evolved for* SUSAN TERHUNE NUNN. *Following college, she was a stewardess for United Airlines. This was during the time when flying was an event, not an ordeal. This was also the time that when you married, that was the end of that career. Susan and husband Jim live on Whidbey Island and have two sons, each with a wife and two daughters. She is a volunteer at Admiralty Head Lighthouse and for the Whale Center in Langley. She writes poetry and short stories and always writes her first drafts with pencil and paper. Her work appears in four anthologies by the Whidbey Writers Group and an anthology of Humor. She has placed in the poetry genre at Whidbey Island Writers Conference and in the "Spirit of Writing" contest. She is currently Residency Assistant for the Northwest Institute of Literary Arts.*

THE NOT SO BLUSHING BUXOM BRIDE

We could hear the roar approaching, and soon they skidded to a stop just outside the Admiralty Head Lighthouse. They were in a black full-bed Dodge Ram V-8 truck. Between the bride and groom peered a dainty little dog. A curly-haired foo-foo type black dog. I waved to them from the lighthouse dining room window. It was past 5 P.M., and our docent shift was supposed to end at five. One of us worked in the gift shop, while the other was host or hostess to greet and answer questions of visitors. We were aware that there was to be a wedding at 5:30 P.M. We also were told two wedding volunteers, docent helpers, would arrive around five. We awaited their guidance since neither of us had ever attended a lighthouse wedding, let alone assisted at one.

At quarter after five, there was still no one else in sight. We decided we should at least invite the bride and groom inside. The couple with dog climbed the stairs past the **PETS MUST WAIT OUTSIDE** sign. They were dressed nicely, coordinated in black and white, including little Pepae or Pepe. I wasn't exactly sure which was the miniature poodle's name. Pepae or Pepe had on a black jacket of sorts with tail (his own, of course). He also wore a white bowtie. We learned he was to be the ring-bearer. Just how he would carry and present the ring, we didn't yet know. The groom, with thinning gray hair, appeared older than his bride. He wore a black suit, white shirt, and silk tie in striped shades of gray. The bride wore an extremely scooped-necked flowing black dress with crocheted white jacket. Numerous sparkly necklaces draped her tanned neckline. She was suspiciously tan considering it was early June, and she had just come down from Alaska. She appeared assertive and in control of the situation, in spite of the lack of usual participants for a wedding.

Soon the minister arrived, but no guests, and still no wedding assistants. We introduced ourselves and learned that the minister was from our local Juan de Fuca church. It appeared that he had not previously met the bride and groom. He joined in the conversation so I slipped away to call the Lighthouse director and find out the names of the current wedding helpers. The director didn't answer, and all I got was the harsh reality of technology and "Leave a message, please." I was thinking, *OK, so now what?*

I returned to the group, and the other docent and I joined in making casual conversation to cover up our apprehension. Meanwhile, since there appeared to be no other guests arriving, the bride turned to us and said, "Oh, by the way could you two be our witnesses?"

I looked at my co-volunteer for approval, then down at my faded jeans and worn docent denim shirt and replied, "Well I'm not exactly dressed for it, but certainly we can do that."

Oh, yes, I failed to mention that this wedding was to take place in the lantern-house tower. This meant thirty steps up a cast-iron spiral staircase ending in an even steeper metal ladder. It had rained that morning and our lighthouse tower roof had a leak, so the steps were damp and slippery. The floor at the bottom was wet, but had a drain. I had swept away most of the water, but couldn't get it all. I was glad the bride didn't have a full-length flowing gown.

Anyhow, back to the dilemma of delay. The fastest way to learn the names of the coordinators was to ask the bride. *How embarrassing! I really didn't want to do that, as we should have known their names.* Again, I slipped away to make a call and inform my husband that I would be home late as I was needed to be a wedding witness. By then the planned five-thirty wedding time had slipped away.

I did finally make contact with one of the co-ordinators. She informed me that she had encountered problems, but would be there in less than ten minutes. However, by that time the assertive buxom bride, groom with striped shades of gray tie, and bowtied dog ring-bearer had decided to proceed with the cozy tower ceremony. I was starting to climb up the tower steps when one of the wedding helpers arrived. As I turned to go down and brief her, I noticed a small strip of material caught on one of the steps, no doubt a piece of the bride's dress. I guessed it was either tear the dress or drop the dog!

I briefed the arriving docent about the situation. She said she would go up the tower to be a witness. By this time, I really wanted to participate, as I was so curious about how Pepae or Pepe was going to present the ring. However, since the lantern-house space is very limited, I felt it best for me to simply slip away.

I was driving out the one-lane staff-only light-house access road as the second tardy docent was driving in. I noticed she had a dog with her, so I waved her down to advise her about the situation, and especially the ring-bearer. She of course was in a hurry so that she could catch up with the ceremony or whatever else had to be tended to. I noticed that her dog was a Shih Tzu. As I drove toward home, I couldn't help but wonder, *How did Pepae or Pepe present the ring?* I felt some disappointment, that after all our apprehension, I didn't get the opportunity to participate in such a unique occasion. I also wondered, as I passed Penn Cove Veterinary Clinic, *What do you suppose a Shih Tzu poo would look like?*

Later I learned the rest of the story. The wedding ceremony was interrupted when the four-legged ring-bearer got excited, and ran around in the tower wagging his tail. The ring was attached to his doggie jacket on a tiny white satiny pillow. His movement prompted the diamond-encrusted ring to work its way loose and clink down the ladder and all thirty metal steps.

The horrified bride screamed, "Oh, my God, no!"

The frantic groom and one wedding docent scrambled down the spiral staircase to search for the elusive ring while the bride nervously watched from above. With overwhelming relief they soon located the ring. They climbed back up, the groom securely holding the ring. The ceremony continued, the bride beamed, and Pepae or Pepe was restrained by a docent.

Just another delightful day at Admiralty Head Lighthouse, where you never know what surprise the next visitor may bring. The other docents and I hope that the trio will live happily together, forever.

GHOSTS OF FORT CASEY

Seventeen steps to nowhere
cracked gray cement bunkers
stories of soldiers past
trusting heavy metal
long ago locked doors
rusting away memories
sounds of cannons
echo in my mind
smell of gunpowder
curls up through my nose
dandelions stand at attention
lined up in the cracks saluting
creeping vines crawl
cling to cement walls
quiet embraces me
holds me here stock still
as I stare into dark
empty hallways of history
drifting fog sweeps across
late afternoon sun
shadows more gray
on decaying fort walls
a cool breeze eases
the austerity of it all
doors to past history
secured – lock me out
foghorn blast from the ferry
brings me back

GOODBYE GARDEN

Dry tired dirt holds persistent weeds
that sway today in quiet breeze
one row of red and yellow dahlias
the only soldiers left standing
one lonely sweet-meat squash
grown from a forgotten seed
hugs the dry empty brown earth
no wooden poles with clinging beans
no string stretched to mark the rows
and show us where the carrots grow
no red-veined beet leaves
Yukon gold potatoes gone
no more pungent onion smell
or creamy white garlic buds
or lime-green lettuce leaves
the raspberry canes remain
the worn wire fence to keep rabbits out
    no need for that
    no need to kneel
    and pull the weeds
    no seeds were planted
    early last spring

ZEBRAS AT DAWN

Zebra-striped socks at 6 A.M.
purple PJ pants   moss green trench coat
heavy fog drifts across West Beach Road

I drive our silver gray Camry
through the damp gray-on-gray fog
headed for the Sea-Tac Shuttle stop

unusual for me to see this time of day
quiet Highway 20 at early dawn
caution warns   watch for deer

conversation lags –

last-minute things spin in my mind
"Do you have your boarding pass
sunglasses Grisham book   pills?"

parked we sit and stare
at the blank back door
of Coupeville Country Store

another car rumbles in
over the gravel approach
joins us in waiting

"It will be an experience
something different to do."
the bus arrives five minutes late

my husband steps swiftly out
I want to bid him goodbye and safe trip
so I'll have to get out of the car

I tighten my green raincoat
brush back my fly-away gray hair
look down at my zebra socks
purple pajama pants pink and gray shoes
and pray *"Please let there be no one I know!"*

THREE DOVE MORNING

Asleep at the edge of the woods
heads tucked into iridescent gray feathers
until the chickadees chirp them awake
then the juncos jump into the fray
as they flurry about the feeder
chase each other away

doves now wander below
they know some seeds will fall
robins ring the stone birdbath
rabbits have worn a path to protection
quail have chosen not to join us this year
we miss their bouncing top-knots

a flicker and downy woodpecker
take turns stabbing the suet
red-wing blackbirds appear
flaunting their bright red stripe
my window frames each changing scene
the starlings arrive as a gang

I bang on the window to frighten them away
the spotted flicker is not afraid
he remains munching his morning seed
two of the doves have skittered into the woods
one remains
could this be the one labeled – lonesome

he perches on the edge of the birdbath
head bowed toward the bowl
could it be – he sees
another feathered friend

Suzanne Fulle

SUZANNE GOODSON FULLE (1929-2015) *was born and raised in Houston, Texas. She graduated from Rice University and attended Columbia Teacher's College in New York City, where she studied with Pearl Buck. She married Floyd Fulle, attorney at law, and moved to Seattle, where she published* Lanterns for Fiesta, *a novel about a Mexican-American family in Houston.* Lavinia *is the first chapter of an unpublished historical novel based on the life of her great-great-great-great-grandparents of North Carolina, Tennessee, and Louisiana during and after the American Revolution.*

LAVINIA

Chapter 1

In the spring of 1771, when I was eight years old, I went alone into Guilford Town with my father. It was the only time in my life I went anywhere alone with Papa.

I had a toothache and all of Mama's home remedies, cloves and camphor especially, hadn't helped a bit. Papa said he'd gotten tired of no one getting any sleep at night because I whimpered and howled. He'd heard about a new tooth-puller who'd set up in town.

Papa was just too soft-hearted to pull it himself.

He said he'd pulled teeth in all the older kids and announced he wouldn't do it with the young ones. The thought of going to town with Papa caused me to ignore the final result as much as possible.

Daddy stood and hunched up his shoulders as he escaped out the door.

"Well, all right then, Lavinia," Mama sighed. "I suppose the little boys can help me down at the creek. And you, Robert," Mama caught Daddy as he hurried down the front path, "do not get tangled up with those Regulators! You know full well how they feel! They want to fight and nothing you or Reverend Caldwell say will make them any mind! You men just need to get back to work!"

Daddy scurried off down the path to the barn for the mule. He looked like Mama's words were falling right on his back.

I pulled my pinny apron over my head and smoothed down my dress, picked up my brogans and pulled my stockings from the line by the fireplace. Then I started after Daddy.

Mama grabbed me and turned me around to face her. She smiled at the happy look on my face. "You better wash up and comb that hair. We don't want Mr. Farris to see you looking like a little heathen."

Her blue eyes sparkled as she pulled me to her. Just looking at her made me smile even more. She was like a doll Big Sister had, round above and round below. Daddy said she was the prettiest girl in seven states when he married her in Virginia. Of course that was a long time before they moved down here to

North Carolina and had us nine children.

There was a rattle in the front yard, and with my shoes and stockings in my hands I ran out to the wagon. Daddy lifted me onto the wagon seat, swung himself up, and with a chirp and a flick of the reins, we rolled down to the gate. Herc, our mule, stopped without being told. He knew more than I did about going to town.

I waved to my big brothers out in the corn patch while Daddy climbed down to open the gate. The big boys caught my little dog Punch as he yipped past them trying to catch up with me.

My two littlest brothers ran up from chunking rocks in Reedy Fork when they heard the rattling of the wagon. Mama had walked down to the creek to help my big sisters with the washing. She hung the shirt she'd washed over the bushes by the creek, wiped her hands on her apron, and followed the little boys to where we waited in the wagon.

Under her sunbonnet Mama's face was red from the North Carolina sun and she squinted her eyes a little as she came. She caught the little boys' hands and held the boys close to her plump side. Even though the boys were four and six years old they loved to have Mama cuddle them, just like we all did.

"We want to go too!" they shouted.

Mama rubbed the boys' curly blond hair. "No, you little 'uns stay here with me. Daddy has to bring back lots of seed. We're already late getting it into the ground with all that's been going on."

Mama adjusted her chiffon mimosa shawl around my chin and pulled her sunbonnet down over my forehead. "Be careful, Lavinia. Hold on tight! Put on your shoes when you get to town!" She kissed Daddy on the forehead. Daddy laughed as he flicked the reins and Herc started up. "Prettiest girl in Virginia," he said, as usual.

I tried not to look too happy because the little boys were not coming. It was my job to take care of them and it was very seldom that I escaped.

The air smelled fresh. Suppose it rained! But Daddy just put his head back, glanced up at the cloudy sky and said, "There's enough blue for a Dutchman's pants!"

I cuddled against Daddy. Our family was big – three sisters and six brothers – and to find a place near Daddy just to get close enough to smell the wool of his coat and the salty odor of his body was hard to do. I loved to look up into his sunburned face at his thin blond hair and into his blue eyes. He was bigger and stronger than anybody else I knew.

I glanced back at my home before we turned the bend by Reedy Fork. The house stood tall in the front and shorter behind, all by itself in the field where our road ended. The house looked as if it had grown out of the dirt. Its logs were brown as oak trees in winter.

We rode along Reedy Fork between laurel and pine trees that scraped each side of the wagon.

Mama was always after Daddy and the boys to widen the road, but Daddy said he had lots more important things to do. A wider road would just make it easier for the tax collectors to find the house. Tax collectors came all the time, which is one of the things Daddy's Regulators hated so much.

We soon reached the little log cabin Presbyterian Church where we attended services on the Sundays when we didn't go into Guilford. I loved the way the cabin nestled in the huge oaks and rhododendrons. Mama said sure a kirk is its people, that it didn't matter how it looked, but I loved the way it looked the most.

Daddy stopped the wagon in front of the church and climbed down to talk to a group of men standing on the bare dirt. They were mostly young men, near my big brothers' ages, but my big brothers didn't hang around with them much. The town Regulators never seemed to do any work, and Mama didn't like that.

Daddy vanished out of sight into the kirk. *Oh, please don't let him stay too long!* I begged Providence. My tooth hurt! Sometimes when Daddy went into the kirk, he didn't come back for hours! But for once Daddy came right back and climbed into the wagon and clucked to Herc. "The Reverend isn't here. Already at the meeting in Guilford."

Farther down the road we passed the fields of our nearest neighbors on Reedy Fork. "Daddy," I began.

"Hm?" Daddy was silent. He rode with his elbows on his bony knees staring at Herc's dark rump before him.

"Why are you looking for Reverend Caldwell? Is something wrong?"

Daddy glanced at me. "Where'd you get an idea like that?"

"Well, Mama and the big girls said that if the

Reverend and the Regulators don't quit arguing there's going to be heck to pay!"

"Well, there's gonna be heck to pay if those Regulators don't listen to the Reverend, I'll tell you that. And I agree with him. Impatient! The Reverend and I and most of the others at the kirk want to take every road we can to get some agreement. The last thing we want is to go into battle!"

"Do the Regulators want to fight?" I sat closer to Daddy.

"Well, not all of them. Most of us think Governor Tryon will finally listen to our petitions. He must know we can't have the sheriff or his men being sent out every day by Fanning to collect more taxes. There's got to be some order here."

"Fanning?" I knew who he was. Clerk of the Court. I'd heard that often enough. But I wanted to hear the rest of it. No one ever told me anything. I just had to pick up information by listening around.

"County Clerk! Has to pass on any petition we send to Governor Tryon. Sometimes I think that weasel Fanning must not be giving those petitions to Tryon. If we could just give them to him ourselves, we'd be better off. Reverend Caldwell is probably meeting Fanning in Guilford right now to give him some more petitions. Something's got to be done before these hotheads get the bit in their teeth."

Daddy gave an angry flick to the reins and Herc came awake. We began to move right along until Herc settled down again.

"Daddy?" I pulled his shirt sleeve almost out of his jerkin, "Can I ask you one more thing?"

" 'May I!' Yes, sure."

"What does Regulator mean?"

Daddy was silent for a few minutes as we jogged along. "Well, how can I explain it to you? You remember when Mama was teaching you to use the loom? How she showed you to step back and then forward? Well, she was regulating the thread and the machine. That means getting it all to work together. The Regulators think they are improving our lives."

"I never have learned how exactly my weaving could improve, but she says I'm better!"

"Yes, well, there are certain rules about weaving, just like there are certain rules about taxing. All we want is to regulate the rules so we know just how much we owe and when we're gonna have to pay. As it is now, anybody can come by and collect. Sometimes the sheriffs collect when people have already paid."

"Mama said that Mrs. Olson's cow was taken the other day! And she'd already paid one tax.'

"By God! Sorry, Livvy, but when that poor woman lost her cow, she was the same as being turned out to starve. I heard about that. It's a good thing someone at the kirk had a cow they could lend her for a while. We'll keep her and her kids alive, but no thanks to Fanning!"

We rode in silence along the creek. As we got nearer town there were more cleared fields and more houses on the uphill side of Reedy Fork.

I loved the houses painted white! Some new people coming into North Carolina painted the logs of their cabins with whitewash. "Look Daddy, aren't those houses pretty?"

"Tories!" Daddy snorted. He flicked the reins at Herc.

"Tories!"

"You know what they are!" Daddy frowned. "They're people who think everything the Brits do is wonderful! Not us Scots. Well, maybe some of those fancy-dancy Royal Scots highlanders do. But we had enough of that bunch back in Ireland."

"Mama said those white houses are like ones in Virginia where she came from, so some people live in houses like that that aren't Tories!"

"Ha!" was all Daddy would say.

I pulled Mama's mimosa shawl out a little so it could be seen as we passed more houses. If we lived near town, I'd wear this shawl every day, even though it wasn't warm enough to wear as a coat, and I'd live in a white house with green shutters.

It was nearly noon, the sun straight overhead, when we reached Guilford town. It wasn't a very big town, but it was where the stores were.

It was so hot that I was glad Mama had put her sunbonnet on me. None of us girls at the kirk liked to wear sunbonnets.

We drove down a dirt road into Guilford. I quickly picked up my heavy brogan shoes and put them on. I looked around at the small buildings built in and out of the woods, at Farris's wooden store front, the tavern, the Ordinary, and the feed store. On the other side of the road, a cooperage and a blacksmith shop stood in a clearing.

The banker was hooking up a muslin against

the sun. Most of the buildings were tied together by new wooden walkways and railings. The steps up to the Ordinary where people could stay the night were full of men, smoking and spitting tobacco into the grass.

Daddy tied Herc to the peeled log railing and lifted me down. "I see Reverend Caldwell over there. Can you walk up and down the boardwalk – maybe go in the drygoods store for a minute? I have to catch the Reverend before he sees Fanning. Then we'll find the tooth-puller. It's not hurting you too much right now, is it?"

"No, but if Mr. Farris has any baby chicks," I grabbed Daddy' s sleeve, "can I get two for the little boys?" I was already feeling guilty at leaving them.

Daddy didn't answer. He waved to a group of men who were sitting on the railings; then he went down to them, forgetting all about me. Some of the men spat in the dust. Others waited in split-cane chairs lined up along the wall. I watched Daddy join them. Reverend Caldwell came out of the hotel and stood beside Daddy. I could see Clerk Fanning looking through the window. He did have a weaselly look like Daddy said. Mama said "You'd have to watch that Fanning in a henhouse."

I recognized some of the town Regulators. There were many men in town who belonged to our Regulators besides the ones at our Church.

Some of them came to our Alamance Church once in a while when Reverend Caldwell was preaching. That was because Reverend Caldwell was the best preacher in the territory. He was also the preacher at Buffalo Creek Presbyterian Church, where we went sometimes.

Reverend Caldwell read petitions that he and Daddy and some of the others had written, but Sunday after Sunday the same petitions were discussed, and Governor Tryon didn't pay any attention. Daddy said Tryon was too busy spending a fortune on Tryon's Palace down near the coast to care about the people around Alamance.

"All this talk is going to lead to trouble!" Mama moaned every Sunday after service on our way home in the wagon. "What's going to keep those Regulators from coming into Guilford and starting a fight like they did last year at Hillsborough? Remember how they burned down Fanning's house?"

Daddy never answered Mama when she talked like that. He just flicked the reins and Herc would step it up a little.

"You know I agree with you on principle." Mama would hold her bonnet feathers with one hand and the buggy handle with the other as we speeded up.

Mama went on: "Those British just want their profits out of the Colonies, and if we don't like it, we can move on. I don't think Tryon even reads those petitions!"

Mama's lips would quiver and she'd turn around on the seat to swat at the little boys who were always scuffling behind her. "Stop that! Behave yourselves! Don't you know this is God's day? You'll ruin your good clothes!"

Now I sighed and climbed the high steps to the

boardwalk. The brogans were too tight on my feet, and my skirt was shorter than was proper for a girl eight years old, I thought. My brothers would have teased me if they'd been there.

I fingered one of the gourd birdhouses hanging along the walls and then pushed open the curtain door to Farris's. I held the deerskin curtain so it wouldn't flap and scare the hens and chicks in the big baskets.

There was a white hen and five yellow chicks like puff balls in a Cherokee basket near the counter. When I stooped to touch them, my tooth gave such a twinge that I sat back on my heels under my full apron and yelped.

"What's the matter there, Lavinia?" Mike Farris stuck his tousled red head over the counter. His freckled face was dusted with flour.

"My tooth!"

Mike came around and made me open my mouth, "Yep, there it is. I thought you was being mighty quiet. Here to see the new tooth-puller?"

"Uh-huh."

"Well, he ain't here. Rode out this morning. Says he ain't staying around, waiting for the British and them Regulators to tangle."

I pressed my hand against my cheek and felt the tears coming.

Mike watched me. "Well," he said, "there ain't anything that painkiller can do that I can't. Come on, Lavinia, let me set you up here."

He lifted me onto the counter. My jaw felt as if one half of my whole face was gonna break right off.

"First thing, you have a sip of this." Mike poured a little pewter cup full of moonshine. I knew what it was because Daddy and his brothers sometimes took it out by the pump when they felt sick. But I was a baptized Presbyterian!

"I can't," I moaned. "I'm pledged teetotal."

"Hell's bells!" Mike said. "This is a special dispensation!"

He tipped my head back and poured some acid-tasting stuff down my throat that felt so bad it made me cough. I was so confused that I hardly even noticed when Mike stuck his pliers into my mouth and with a jerk and a twist, pulled out my tooth, the second from the left at the bottom.

Mike wiped my face with a clean flour sack and lifted me down. He held a bucket for me to spit blood, then opened my mouth and put a bit of cleaned cotton into the hole where the tooth had been. I was as wobbly as a new calf, but I managed to get out the door and onto the bench before I collapsed.

Reverend Caldwell drove his buggy down the dirt road past Farris's and didn't even see me. Daddy came along the wooden sidewalk waving his arms, and turned to shout back at the men. "Not yet! We have to give it another shot! You want a war? You do, huh? How much ammunition you got? Well, I'll see you at the kirk tonight, seven."

He turned to me, his face red. "Ready?"

"Uh-huh."

He hoisted me into the wagon and climbed up himself. Then he backed Herc out and we started on our way home without another word.

"You get the seed?" I mumbled past the cotton in my mouth.

"Oh, my Lord!" Daddy turned the wagon around again, "Forgot. And weren't we going to do something about your tooth?"

I handed him my tooth wrapped in a bit of flour sack and sat up straight beside him on the seat.

"How – where?" But Daddy was too distracted to pursue it as he slowed Herc, then got out and tied him up again.

I sat, my tooth forgotten, and watched Daddy's hunched back as he went into Farris's store. Something was very wrong when Daddy didn't remember us kids.

It had something to do with the angry young Regulators who watched us from the porch rail. As I looked back, one of them raised his fist at me.

Kaye LaTorra Erickson

MARY KATHERINE LATORRA ERICKSON (1925-2012),
*known as Kaye, was a charter member of Whidbey Writers
Group. When she retired as a registered nurse at Whidbey
General Hospital, she wrote medical articles for newspapers
and technical publications. Then, from her home at Long Point
near Coupeville where she lived with her husband Harvey in
retirement, she turned to fiction writing. Her stories and
poems have appeared in all seven of the earlier WWG
anthologies. Her story "Bitch" won first place in the Memoir
category of the 2006 "Spirit of Writing" contest sponsored by
the Whidbey Island Writers Association.*

BITCH

She couldn't make a sound but there was no
doubt what she had said. Seven years of Intensive
Care Nursing, handling patients with tubes down
their throats to aid their breathing by keeping the
vocal cords apart and the patient voiceless had made
me a proficient lip-reader.

"Bitch," she mouthed again. The tape holding
the tube in place pulled her lips back in a snaggle-
toothed, menacing grin. "Oh great," I told myself,
"another tough old dame from the streets." We saw

so many needful patients in those days that I was growing jaded.

"OK, OK, just take it easy." I spoke the usual platitudes as I surveyed the filthy, emaciated woman lying in the Coronary Care bed. "You've had a heart attack. I'm your nurse. My name is Kaye."

"Bitch, bitch," she mouthed around the breathing tube as she struggled against the wrist restraints.

My inner voice spoke to me, "Well, I'm not too crazy about you either, lady." My out loud nurse's voice continued with the usual attempt to establish patient rapport. "It's OK. I'm here to help you. We have your arms tied so you won't pull all the tubes out. You're better but you had a big heart attack and need the breathing tube a while longer." I talked as I gathered bath basin and towels from the counter.

She lay watching my every move. The monitors told me she was a very sick lady but doing well. The medications were working and the respirator was giving her good deep breaths.

She was so fragile. Her skin, delicate as parchment, was gray with embedded dirt. Deeply sunken brown eyes darted around the room, wary as a fox. Two rotting snags in her lower gum were all the teeth she seemed to have. A spider's web of scant, fine gray hair which, I felt certain, harbored a colony of lice, lay tangled about her head. I checked her chart. Her name was Rose. She was sixty-eight and looked eighty.

"Rose, I'm going to give you a bath, get you all clean and comfortable." I placed my hand gently over hers. A sudden volcanic upheaval happened as the bundle of bones and dehydrated flesh began to twist and writhe against the restraints and her lips formed the word "bitch" over and over again.

I feared for her safety. She didn't need this sort of agitation after such a heart attack. I reached for my tube of intravenous medications.

"I'm going to give you something to relax you and let you sleep." I injected the paralyzing and sleeping agents into her intravenous line.

My inner voice spoke. "You tough old dame, who do you think you are? This job is hard enough without this kind of crap. Bitch yourself. I'm going to get you clean whether you like it or not. You're not going to fight me so hard you have another coronary and code on my shift." I slipped a paper surgical cap over her hair and she looked almost angelic sleeping so peacefully.

After a third basin of bath water and much gentle scrubbing, I managed to remove most of the dirt and odor. Rose slept quietly. I slipped her arms out of the restraints, one at a time, and turned my final attention to her hands and arms.

I scrubbed her right hand and trimmed the long yellowed nails. After retying that restraint I went to work on the left arm. As I turned the hand palm up, I saw what appeared to be a dark streak of dirt, midline, about two inches above the wrist. I scrubbed, and scrubbed again.

Crudely tattooed blue numbers became visible. I had read about it, seen documentaries and movies, but never had I touched a concentration camp survivor. I stood gazing at this woman, this "tough old dame" now in my care. I held her fragile hand in mine and traced the blue tattoo with my finger.

I spoke with my out loud nurse voice again. "Rose, I'm sorry." I knew she couldn't hear me but I needed to say it. "You're safe here. We want to help you get well."

I left her to sleep on the medications I had given her. My sympathy roused me to the point of tears. I turned my attention to her records. Leaning against the supply cabinet so I could keep a good eye on Rose and all her equipment, I read the admit notes.

The emergency room nurse who had admitted her last evening had charted, "This patient appears very frightened. She keeps repeating the word *bitte*, which, if my high school German does not fail me, means *please*."

Authors' Publications

BARB BLAND has published a memoir, *Running Free,* about turning a feral dog into a household pet. Her poems "Berry Battle" and "Apricot Evening" were published in the Whidbey Island Writers Association's *In the Spirit of Writing 2012* and *2013* magazines, respectively.

PAT KELLEY BRUNJES has published a book of poetry, *Poetry from the Desert Floor,* and is working on her first novel.

CAROL CARNAHAN has published two pieces in an anthology about a Nature Conservancy Preserve titled "Zumwalt: Writings from the Prairie," and an article in *Mushing Magazine,* "Can Sled Dogs Help Cure Cancer?" She was a winner in a Seattle Times writing contest called *Misadventures in Travel.*

MIKO JOHNSTON is halfway through completing a series of historical novels. Her first, *A Petal In The Wind,* published by Champlain Avenue Books, is currently available. *A Petal In The Wind II* is scheduled for publication in fall of 2015. Her short story, "By Anonymous," was published in the Sisters In Crime anthology *Last Exit to Murder.*

GORDON M. LABUHN has published two mystery novels: *Murder Has Two Faces* and *Murder Has Three Faces*; a memoir, *My Gang*; and the story "Roxanne" in the anthology *The Dog With the Old Soul*. His story "My Woman Elizabeth" was the First Place prize-winner in the Bayview, Washington, Classic Car Show Writing Competition.

MIKE MCNEFF'S published works include the novels *GOTU, Necessary Retribution,* and *Hard Justice,* and several short stories.

NASUS NUNN has placed in the poetry genre at Whidbey Island Writers Conference, in the Whidbey Island Writers Association's "Spirit of Writing" contest, and in the *Writer's Digest* Contest 2011.

SANDRA MCGILLIVRAY ORTGIES has written numerous regional articles for a Navy travel magazine, *The Military Beat*, as well as local interest features for the *Coupeville Examiner* and the *South Whidbey Record*. Over the years, she has placed in four categories in the Whidbey Island Writers Association's writing contest.

DOROTHY READ's short stories have appeared in Whidbey Writers Workshop's *Soundings Review;* Adams Media's *The Rocking Chair Reader: Family Gatherings* and *Coming Home; Sea of Voices, Isle of Story* from Triple Tree Press; and four of the Whidbey Writers Group anthologies. With Ilse Evelijn Veere Smit, she co-authored the book *End the*

Silence, a full-length memoir of a woman who survived the Japanese occupation of the Dutch East Indies (now Indonesia) during WWII and the bloody revolution that followed.

AVIS RECTOR has published a children's book *Carl Helps on the Farm;* and a novel, *Pauline, A New Beginning on Whidbey Island.*

KAREN ROTHBOECK is currently seeking representation for her first book, a science fiction novel.

LARRY SHAFER has published an article in *Seattle Magazine,* "The Reese Case Reappraised," about an off-duty police officer who shot and killed an African-American after a brawl in a Chinatown restaurant. His guest column, "Bush abuses his authority in firing U.S. attorneys," was published in the *Seattle Post-Intelligencer.*

ROWENA WILLIAMSON has published the novels *Escape to the Highlands; MacGregor's Bargain; MacGregor's Odyssey; Ryan and the Redhead;* and *Ryan and the Redhead and the White Hag.*

BILL WILSON has published a literary science fiction novella, *Stowaway,* about a writer who literally got into the head of a space-tug navigator on his way to Mars.

Answers to the puzzle on page 171.

				8			
1	B	I	**R**	T	H		
2	I	N	F	**A**	N	T	
3	Y	O	U	**T**	H		
4	A	D	U	L	**T**		
5	E	**L**	D	E	R		
6	D	**E**	A	T	H		
7	E	T	E	**R**	N	A	L